# ROGUE'S LEGACY

# ROGUE'S LEGACY

## L. L. Foreman

GUNSMOKE

This hardback edition 2011
by AudioGO Ltd
by arrangement with
Golden West Literary Agency

ISBN 978 1 408 46313 0

British Library Cataloguing in Publication Data available.

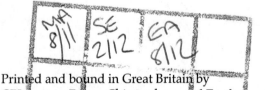

Printed and bound in Great Britain by
CPI Antony Rowe, Chippenham and Eastbourne

# I

Rain must have fallen up in the mountains, probably a spring cloudburst, heavy enough for the run-off to bring flash floods down here in the arroyos of this parched border country. The river, usually a low trickle, was now a torrent bearing the flotsam of uprooted trees and brush. Even the shallows on the sand spits ran knee keep, creating stumbling impediments to a hasty crossing on horseback.

Blowing hard, the three horses splashed over to the ragged line of the north bank. They had done well, after their straining effort of racing up from the south without much of a breather. Two of them, a long-legged black and a hard-mouthed brute of a sorrel, scrambled up the slippery clay shelf onto dry land. Streaming water, they crashed on into the brasada thickets that hugged the river. Their riders ducked, upraised arms shielding their faces from the poisoned thorns of high and graceful green-and-gold retamas.

The third horse, a sturdy little Moro mare, failed to climb the bank. She had got a bullet and her strength was drained out. The swirling water showed pink streaks where she floundered for footing. A floating log cruelly struck her hindquarters. The mare uttered a thin squeal before her head went under, and the rushing current of the swollen river took possession; it swept the mare and her rider in a rolling tangle away from the bank.

The two riders ahead, hearing the frantic squeal of the mare, reined fast about and swung back through the punishing brush. They didn't exchange a word or glance, being of one accord, to return to their downed companion.

The rider of the long-legged black had his rope held ready, coiled in his right hand, when he reined to stiff halt on the edge of the riverbank. He threw the rope uncoiling to a small head, wet and dark, that bobbed up in the water.

As he made his cast, he whipped a glance across the river. He saw horsemen breaking into sight here and there coming at a furiously headlong gallop. Well, they had a right to be furious. It was their country: Mexico.

"Grab on and hold tight!" he called to the struggling swimmer, who couldn't swim worth a damn. Few in the Southwest had learned how. No water.

His voice was as harsh as his looks, as icily calm as his deepset gray eyes. His face, strongly muscled, saturnine in its humor, and dark, was the face of a man who had long grown accustomed to running his life to a fast tempo of rough-and-ready danger. The knee-length coat that he wore, black, ministerial, did nothing to soften his appearance. Nor did his black hat, wide of brim and flat-crowned, worn at a rakish slant as if to give the lie to the clerical effect.

He was big, tall. The somber austereness of his garb, the garb of a professional gambler, accentuated his air of leashed power, his go-to-hell toughness. His name was Rogate Bishop, and rumor had it that he might once have been a gentleman. Whatever the truth of the rumor, tempestuous years had buried his early past beyond recall. He was billed as a wanted man in more places than he could remember.

The other man, the rider of the hard-mouthed sorrel, drew up beside Bishop with a wrenching haul on the reins that brought his ornery mount back onto its haunches. He, too, wore the look of danger on his face,

6

and with it an acceptance of danger as a kind of joke. It put a dancing gleam into his eyes.

Birds of a feather ... Wild hawks.

He actually laughed, swinging down from his saddle and plucking his rifle out of its leather boot—although he swayed when his feet hit the ground, as if he had been riding too long and lost his walking legs. And he passed an inconsequential remark that was typical of him.

"Ah, well, the kid probably needed a bath, anyway!"

He braced his rifle against the gnarled trunk of a giant mesquite, taking aim across the river.

"Better drag the tyke out fast, Bishop, never mind the skin. The dons are laying up to shoot!"

Carbines cracked as he ended speaking. The carbines of a squad of Rurales, fearsomely efficient keepers of the peace, gringo-haters for good reasons. They sent up little smoke-balls, stirred rattling echoes over the water, and raised splashes around the small dark head in the river.

The owner of the small dark head caught the thrown end of rope, brushed back a hank of wet hair, and sang out, "Haul away, Rogue!"

Rogate Bishop, gambler, gunfighter, free-lance trouble-shooter, called Rogue Bishop to his face only by his familiars—and they were few, for he was a loner—wasted no time on any gentle hand-hauling. He flipped a turn of the rope around his saddlehorn, spun the black horse, dug in his heels.

The big black lunged ten yards before Bishop reined it in. The kid came skimming out of the river like a reeled-in catfish. Then up the bank, plowing red clay, to lie gasping, spewing water.

"And now," Bishop observed, gathering up his rope, "she could do with another bath. That mud. Must be a full-time job, O'Terran, being a father. I wouldn't take it on. Don't see how you find time for anything else."

The rifle braced against the mesquite trunk began thudding. "Oh, I don't know. Shamrock's a good kid in her way." Captain O'Terran spoke between shots. His face was gray, but it retained a smile, for seriousness wasn't in his nature. "She takes care of herself pretty well, considering. I never pester her about personal—"

Then he went to his knees, not by choice, and fell against the mesquite. Righting himself there on his knees he braced the smoking rifle again.

A quixotic adventurer, Captain O'Terran. An incorrigibly romantic desperado, forever plunging into lost causes and kicking up some lighthearted trouble of his own between-times. He was also by way of being a professional Irishman, full of blarney, indulging in an exaggerated brogue when the whim struck him or when charm was needed to wriggle out of scrapes.

His title of Captain was sheer vanity. He had picked it up during a brief period of skippering a gun-running lugger for some Central American revolutionists whose cause appealed to him. The head revolutionists had sold out and decamped overnight, leaving him stranded with the leaky old lugger.

His handsome face was sunken now. Blood darkly splotched the front of his shirt. This was one scrape when blarney and charm couldn't turn the trick. But the gallant pose, necessary to his self-esteem, had to be sustained. So he smiled while working the rifle, believing his gaunt grimace to be gayly devil-may-care.

One of his bullets fell far too short, which was a rare occurrence, he being a crack shot. He swayed on his knees, swore softly, and fumbled fresh shells from his pocket, dropping a couple of them.

"Shamrock, me darlin' daughter, come here!" he called, the rich and lilting brogue as false as his smile. He shoved the rifle and shells uncertainly in the direction of his young daughter. "Show the dons how you can shoot, eh? I got mud in me eye an' can't see clear. Keep your sweet eye on yon *mogote* downriver, it's their best bet to try a crossing."

He twisted around to send Bishop his ghastly smile. "Do we make a stand here, Mr. Bishop, or is it your preference to travel on?"

Before replying, Bishop got settled down with his own rifle. He took aim, fired, and levered a fresh shell into the breech. A riderless horse broke from the brush on the south bank, skittered at the river's edge, and bolted back.

O'Terran's sorrel horse stood shivering in plain sight, unlike Bishop's black. It was like O'Terran to neglect simple precaution. A wonder he had stayed alive this long. Luck of the Irish; nothing else could account for it, Bishop thought. A scattery blast of return fire from over the river sent the sorrel to hopping aimlessly about, squealing. Another blast and it collapsed, the creak of strained leathers sounding like dry wood breaking.

Bishop then spared a glance at O'Terran's face. "We might as well stick it out here for a spell, now we've made a halt," he replied. "Only one horse left for the three of us." Two of us, he privately amended.

Shamrock O'Terran used her father's rifle expertly. The Captain had taken pains to educate her in skills that were not commonly required of a young girl. She, too, paid a look to the gray, sunken face. She could read the signs that said this was Captain O'Terran's last halt. But she betrayed no more knowledge of the fact than did Bishop. You didn't make any mawkish display over a dying man, even though the man was your father, only kin, champion, your god . . .

You didn't let him see that you knew, let alone intrude on him. A man owned the right to privacy at such a time. Decent considerateness. Time for a reflective summing-up of his life, a gathering of inner resources so that he could step off the end of his road without stumbling too badly.

So the kid, Shamrock, blinked only furtively, careful to keep her tears unseen, and fired with concentrated animosity at the big-hatted men across the river. And she whistled tunelessly through her teeth, copying the habit of the Captain whenever his back was to the wall.

She was an odd kind of urchin, thought Bishop, hunched beside her, shooting. He put her age at about fifteen, if that. Couldn't be older. Her slim shape . . . Half child, half woman. Her dark blue eyes, almost violet, looked too large for her face; they didn't tell anything definite about her. They contained a mingling of melancholy and joyousness, fierce moods and gentle pensiveness. One could never foretell, if an enemy fell into her hands, whether she would kill with a swift stroke or forgive and kiss him for his helplessness.

"Tough little brat!" Bishop mused to himself.

And then another thought pressed upon him. It brought the beginning of a scowl to his hard mouth. Damned bad luck O'Terran had to catch a bullet in the chest; he was going to die, leaving his kid behind. A disturbing prospect. Bishop wanted no part of that burdensome legacy. There just wasn't any room for it in his kind of life.

O'Terran had caught that bullet as they tore through the village of Tierra Blanca, when the squad of Rurales burst from a cantina and ran out at them on the street. He had shot the wrong man. It was the skinny officer who'd had a cocked gun lined dead on him, but O'Terran had picked the big fellow who jumped at the bridle of Shamrock's mare. He wasn't much as a parent, but he did have protective instincts.

Candelaria was where it started, in the biggest gambling house down there on the Mexican end of the old Chihuahua Trail where Yankee traders far from home used to do business in silks and cottons left over from their Santa Fe peddling.

It would always remain a mystery to Bishop why O'terran slugged the flashy monte dealer in the teeth. There hadn't been much opportunity since for explanations. He most likely had a perfectly good reason, monte dealers being what they were, and Bishop didn't hold it against him. The dealer came up off the floor with a silver sleeve-pistol, yelling for friends.

Bishop, comfortably nursing along a run of fair luck at another table, had not been disposed to take part in the resulting riot. Not until he noticed that he and the Irishman happened to be the only gringos in the place. The Irishman had his hands full, battling the monte dealer's friends.

While Bishop was making up his mind, the brat appeared at the front door. She had a lean, lightweight Spanish revolver. Taking in the situation, she proceeded to pop out the lamps, with a cool efficiency that suggested she had performed this service before. She sideswiped senseless an *oficial de policia* who made a lunge at her.

Bishop took a hand then. He had to. The fracas was fast exploding all around him in the half-dark. Several touchy citizens were showing antagonistic designs upon him. The Yankee traders hadn't left a lasting residue of goodwill here, and the actions of certain other gringos—filibusterers and their like—weren't calculated to establish fond international relations.

He scooped up his cash stakes, slammed off two *rancheros* who closed in on him, and drew the pair of heavy guns that he wore under his ministerial coat. International relations suffered another setback.

"Let's get out o' here, Irish!"

They made it to their horses and quit Candelaria in brisk order. Candelaria carried the grudge stubbornly after them. Some of its leading citizens had taken bodily hurt. Others had got their dignity damaged. The gambling house, owned by the *alcalde* himself, would never look quite the same again. Civic pride demanded full justice.

The longer the pursuit lasted, the bigger it grew, new members joining in the hue and cry all along the line, until it seemed to the fugitives that they were rolling up half of Mexico behind them in their race north.

"I'm Captain O'Terran. This is my daughter, Shamrock."

"Rogate Bishop."

"Glad to know you, Mr. Bishop."

"M'mm." Bishop ran a dour look over the raffish pair. A penniless adventurer and his wildcat kid. They spelled trouble.

Well, see them safe over the river, provided it could be reached. Then shake them off. Let them go their busted way. All that saved them from being tramps was possession of a horse apiece, and they had probably stolen them somewhere. Bishop, a loner, hadn't intended to let himself get involved with the pair for any length of time. The river was the deadline. Once the river was crossed, his temporary alliance with them would end. He would go his own way.

But that was before O'Terran stopped a bullet with his chest . . .

## II

Captain O'Terran stretched himself out in the shade of the mesquite, pulling his hat over his eyes as if settling down for a noonday nap regardless of the perilous situation. He had always taken matters lightly, including his responsibilities as a married man. Irishmen, it was said, made good lovers but bad husbands.

His had been a runaway marriage, an elopement and hasty wedding while on the dodge from the bride's furious family and relatives, who knew he wasn't fit for her. He wasn't. Marriage hadn't changed him; it didn't cramp his free spirit nor fetter his far-roving feet. Yet the girl of his choice had never voiced a complaint. She had lived a dully sheltered life before he came. He had shown her a bright, gay, carefree world, she had assured him, the day she died in his arms. Tuberculosis.

Perhaps he was thinking of her now, thinking deeply of her, of his sorry omissions and guiltful transgressions. Good wife, bad husband. He murmured a name that Bishop didn't quite catch. The name wasn't Shamrock—that outrageously blatant Irish name that only a man like O'Terran would think of tagging onto his offspring. Shamrock! What a monicker to give to a girl!

Downriver, a band of riders broke from the *mogote*, as O'Terran had predicted. The *mogote* was a thicket of mesquite and huisache that covered a point of land jutting into the river. The riders charged into the water with a mighty splashing that practically screened them from sight. At the same time, a second group, upriver, began crossing. The detail of an international boundary

13

was having no restraint upon the anger of the Mexicans.

They couldn't be blamed for feeling wrathy, Bishop considered. After all, a visitor to a land not his own should use discretion and behave himself, not go kicking the works apart as he and the O'Terrans had done. Shooting at Rurales was an extremely serious matter. The Rurales were rough-and-ready keepers of the law, given extraordinary power to execute culprits on the spot. Their ranks were filled largely with ex-bandits, very tough hombres whose evaluation of human life ran low.

Bishop had friends and enemies on both sides of the border, and he spread his personal regard over them evenly. He was equally impartial when it came to pursuers who craved to blow his head off. Whoever they were, and whatever their reason, he wasn't going to let them do it if he could help it.

So he fired. "Watch out, or they'll flank us both ways!" he growled.

His heavy-caliber rifle roared its magazine empty. He reloaded fast, slammed two more bullets into the midst of what had become a threshing chaos of men and horses and churning water, and whirled to give his attention to the group attempting to make the upriver crossing.

He wasn't needed much there, though, he found. The kid, steadily sighting her shots, had broken up the danger from that quarter. She grinned one-sidedly at him.

"I'm taking care of that bunch, Rogue!"

The abbreviation of his given name didn't please Bishop. Few people dared the familiarity of calling him Rogue to his face. He wasn't the kind of man to allow people to become easily familiar with him.

"M'mm!" Then gruffly, "Okay." Which was a long step toward tolerance. A fatal step. Abhor, tolerate, embrace: age-old pattern.

He fished into the breast pocket of his coat and found

a Mexican cigar that wasn't too badly crushed for smoking, and crunched its end between his teeth. Chewing on the sweetened tobacco while searching for a dry match, he sat back on his heels, contemplating the south bank. An occasional shot snarled across, but he couldn't see any movement now in the brush over there. For the time being he and the O'Terrans had the best of it. The sharp edge of their pursuers' zeal had got nicked and dulled.

"They're thinking it over," he remarked. He found a dry match in the breast pocket of his coat and lit his cigar. "Probably thinking about fording the river some other place and cutting around behind us. Want a drink, O'-Terran? I've got a bottle in my saddlebag. Tequila."

It was Shamrock who answered him, from where she knelt beside O'Terran, looking down at the sunken face. She had removed the covering hat, and now she replaced it. She was dry-eyed, her expression impenetrable, her tone of voice flat.

"No," she said, "Captain doesn't want a drink, thanks. He's dead."

"Sorry," Bishop said, and could find nothing else to add to that one word.

He took off his hat and gazed into it. Was the kid, he wondered, rawhide all the way through, incapable of emotion? Or was the absence of tears a stringent rule imposed by self-control, a self-control early learned the hard way as the daughter of that fatally unrestrained, improvident Irishman?

Well, no matter, it was a whole lot better than having on his hands an hysterically sobbing girl shattered out of her senses by grief. There was that much to be thankful for.

Then he heard her murmur unsteadily, "Have a good trip, Captain. Give my love to Mother."

At the back of his mind Bishop was already searching

for a solution to the problem of what he was to do with her. A knotty problem. His conscience, tough as it was, refused to accept the easiest answer: desert her, turn her adrift. This was no country for an orphaned girl, a young waif. Hard, hungry country, infested with border-jumpers, degraded renegades, Apaches. She couldn't possibly make her way in it, alone and on foot.

On the other hand, he was thoroughly committed to his kind of haphazard life, by notoriety piled upon preference. He knew perfectly well that he was even less fitted to take a young girl under his wing than O'Terran had qualified as a father. Far less.

"I'll have to take you up behind me on my horse," he told Shamrock, as if needing to explain stern facts to a child. His knowledge of young minds was hazy. He tended to lump all youngsters together in a kind of inferior bracket. " 'Fraid it won't be any too comfortable for you," he warned.

"I've ridden double before," she said, "many a time. Behind Captain. Long rides, some. I don't have a nurse-maid's backside."

He blinked at her plain language. "Then you know what to expect. Hard bumping till we get out of this thrown-away piece of country. Those hombres won't quit here. Their blood's up. I'll make for Union Junction."

"Captain had trouble there, once. A lousy town, that."

"I share your opinion. But Union Junction's way off-bounds to the Rurales, so there's where we head. After we bury—"

She shook her head. "How? Nothing to dig his grave with, only our hands. They'll be all round us. No, we just cover him up, best we can."

"Guess it'll have to do," Bishop said, relieved, "if it's okay with you." He hadn't welcomed the task of scrabbling out a grave while the pursuers forded the river and surrounded them. It would have had to be a shallow grave, anyway; the earth was grouty beneath the sand.

Shamrock nodded her head. She was still dry-eyed. "It's okay. He doesn't—didn't—believe in fancy funerals. I'll take his gun and belt. Waste not, want not, he always said." She smiled ruefully. "If he had practiced what he preached, he might've got rich a dozen times!"

She unbuckled the gunbelt, gently tugged it loose from under her father's body, and strapped it on around her waist. The belt was cumbersome, broad, weighted with looped catridges. She had to pull the tongue of the buckle to its first hole, and even then the holster sagged low.

"You're mighty small to wear that full-size harness," commented Bishop, eyeing her critically. "It'll drag you down."

The kid wore canvas pants, cut off at the bottoms to fit her, more or less. A man's faded flannel shirt, stuffed into the pants, which overlapped at the waist and were held up somewhat precariously by a twisted sash of red silk. Her hat was a Chapala sombrero, too big for her.

A hell of an outfit for an American girl. And muddy from head to foot. She looked like a diminutive bandit who had struck rough going.

"Behind a good gun," she retorted, "I'm as big as you! As big as anybody!"

Bishop held reservations about that statement. It characterized the cocky reasoning that had led many brash sprouts down a short trail to disaster. He couldn't recall ever knowing a girl who subscribed to the suicidal notion. However, this girl stood in a class by herself.

He let it pass, saying, "Let's tend to the Captain."

They heaped up sand and stepped back to look at the mound for a moment: burial place of Captain O'-Terran, adventurer, soldier of fortune, chronic loser.

"Goodby," Shamrock whispered.

Later, when they had left the river behind them,

Bishop said to her, "Soon's I can, I'll pick you up a horse and a decent outfit to wear." He meant it as a promise, kindly enough. Poor kid. Homeless urchin in bedraggled rags.

To his irritation, she instantly got proddy. "What's wrong with what I've got on? Captain gave me these!"

"They're dirty, harum-scarum, not fit to be seen!" he replied, made blunt-spoken by her belligerence.

Despite the ups and downs of his checkered life, he generally managed to wear decent garb and own a good horse. It was against his personal principles to allow himself to go flat broke, though often he came close to it.

He hadn't intended his reply to sound as scathing as it did, but he had a weight on his mind and wasn't in the mood to tone down his speech. Getting Shamrock passably clothed seemed to him to be the first item on the bill. After which, getting rid of her posed the next problem; he had no answer to that at present.

She was riding behind him on the black horse, her hands gripping his coat for security. He couldn't see her bite her lower lip. "I don't take charity!" she said. "Not from you, Rogue Bishop, or anybody else!"

Scowling ahead at sand dunes and clumps of prickly-pear cactus, he rolled his big shoulders as if to ease them of a growing load. "You," he grunted, "will take what I give you! You'll try to look more presentable!"

Nor could he see the quick sparkle of tears in her eyes. Tears of angry shame.

"Captain never found fault with how I look!"

"I'm not the Captain."

"That's for sure!"

"Meaning no insult to him, I'd say he sort of regarded you as a boy. From now on, you're going to look an' act like a girl. It's more natural."

"Oh? We'll see . . ."

Bishop's scowl deepened. A suspicion formed that
the bold Captain O'Terran had let his daughter run wild
because she simply was too much for him and he couldn't
handle her. The brat had a strong mind of her own,
obviously. She didn't respect her elders merely because
they were grown-ups.

That being the case, it posed additional difficulties for
an unwilling guardian. This, he reflected with bleak
humor, was one hell of a spot for him to get into. Rogue
Bishop, foster father of a willful wildcat. A new experience for him, who thought he had seen everything.

Perhaps the best method of tackling the difficulties
was to use guile. Females of any age were susceptible
to soft and beguiling words from a man. They melted,
dropped the cool crust, became yearningly feminine. Yes,
that was the card to play.

"When you're gussied up in a dress and all the fixings,
Shamrock," he remarked craftily over his shoulder to her,
"I bet you're a right fetching girl, pretty as a pic-
ture."

"Save your flattery for dancehall Lulus!" came her fast
retort. "Captain was a master at it. He could wheedle
free bed from a queen!"

So much for that. A wasted effort. The damned kid
was invulnerable. A white savage, hard as granite.

After a while, though, after a long silence between
them, during which Bishop entertained morose thoughts
of the future, Shamrock's gripping hands slid down his
coat. Her arms encircled him. She leaned against him,
her head resting on his back.

"Okay, Rogue. Anything you say. Anything."

There was a tenderly intimate quality in her voice
that caused Bishop to clamp his mouth shut. His bit
of guile had gone a long way, farther than he planned.
It was bearing fresh problems to plague him.

The child-woman behind him, he then realized, was

starved for affection. And she wanted the security of adult discipline, really wanted it, knowing she needed it.

"You're right, Rogue. I'm kind of pretty when I'm dolled up. Can't imagine how you knew it, way I am."

"It shows."

Her arms tightened around him. Her head nuzzled his back.

Great God, he thought, not that! I'm old enough to be her father, near about. Is the kid putting me in her dead father's place? Is she flooding me in the pent-up love that she couldn't give to him? Great God! Don't let it be. I'm too human. I'm a male. She's in the earliest bloom of womanhood. We'll have to night-camp together under my blanket.

"Rogue—" she began.

"Shut up!" he snapped at her. "Don't say anything more! And keep your arms still, and your head!"

"Okay, Rogue."

# III

They off-tracked from Union Junction, due to persistent pursuit, and pulled into Dry Spring instead. Bishop disliked the place; he had passed through it in the past. A desolate huddle of squatty buildings, mostly stone-and-adobe. No hotel, no livery stable. For some obscure reason, probably political, a deputy of the county sheriff resided here—which added to Bishop's prejudice. Still, any port in a storm . . .

The town was well-named. Everything had long gone dry, the spring, all surface water. A few water-holes, fed by wells—there was water beneath the baked surface, if a rancher had the money to pay for deep digging—supported scrubby cattle. The poor range, ten acres to a cow, made cattle-raising meagerly feasible. The sale of lean beef, lean to the muscle, supported Dry Spring.

A hungry little town, poverty-stricken. And being poor it was, of course, the more eager to strike for fortune. There had to be *some* money here. There were always the big ones with money.

Bishop entertained no desire to go shopping for feminine attire. That was Shamrock's province. She was able to do a better job of it than he could. The underthings and all that.

He gave her money, a generous fistful of gold coins, double-eagles, from his money belt. At first she refused to take his money. She protested that she wouldn't take charity, not from anyone.

"Charity, hell!" Bishop blared at her. "Riding with me, you've got to look decent, not lowdown trampish! I don't ride with tramps!"

Flushing, Shamrock accepted the money.

"I'll try to make it up to you, Rogue. Anyway I can. Anyway I can repay you for all you've done—"

"Forget it! Captain O'Terran—your father—left you in my hands! I'm trying to do what's best for you, that's all. Get yourself dressed!"

He was overly harsh with her, because he detected signs that she was putting him in the place of her father. More than that, the damfool kid was falling in love with him. She had loved her father. Her love had to fasten onto somebody, Bishop supposed, and he was the handiest object. In fact, she had nobody else but him; nobody else to be the object of her affection. Beneath her tough crust, the girl was warmly affectionate.

Puppy love.

Then, looking into her eyes, Bishop saw that she was a woman. Or, at any rate, a young female blossoming into the ripeness of womanhood. So young. So vulnerable.

"Don't you have any relatives?" he demanded of her. "Folks who'd take you in and give you a home?"

She shook her head, gazing at him forlornly. "Captain was a black sheep. His family cut him off. Even his brother, a church minister, never answered my note to him, one time we were flat broke in Venezuela. That's a tough country to be broke in!"

"Any place you're broke, it's tough."

"That's true. Broke, nobody's your friend." Her cynicism was too old for her years. She must have had some bad experiences, roaming far and wide with O'Terran. The forlornness of her look deepened to sad resignation. "Don't you want me, Rogue? Just say so and—and I'll go."

He put his arm around her shoulders, hugged her briefly, said gruffly, "We're together, kid!"

Starry-eyed, flushed with happiness, Shamrock set off to buy herself feminine garb. A pretty dress. Frilly underthings. To please him, her man, or at any rate her guardian.

Bishop headed for the only saloon in town, a low-roofed adobe establishment that had a broken window stuffed with rags to keep out the dust. It didn't look promising. At best, it would serve to pass the time while he waited for the girl to get her shopping done. He rolled his broad shoulders uneasily, feeling already shackled to unfamiliar duties and cares.

Gazing back at him, Shamrock smiled. The sign on the saloon was crudely painted, faded colorless by the sun, barely legible, but he had unerringly spotted it. Like the Captain. Bishop was younger than the Captain, she guessed. Not that it mattered if he wasn't. Her life had been spent among grownups, mostly hard-drinking men.

Rogue Bishop, her guardian. The smile on her young face deepened, warming to a soft glow. Her guardian? She would improve that relationship between them. "Wait till I fix myself up pretty," she whispered. "You just wait, Rogue!"

Before going into the saloon, Bishop watered his horse at the wooden trough outside, loosened cinch, aired the saddle blanket. The grainsack was empty; he hoped to be able to buy some grain here, and maybe a horse for Shamrock. He left the black rein-tied at the hitching rack alongside several ribby cow ponies that showed signs of having been overworked and underfed.

The barroom, drearily cheerless, reeked of stale odors. After pausing to adjust his eyes to the gloom, he took note that his entrance had raised a stir of interest, a hush that meant strangers were few and far between in Dry Spring. No wonder, he thought dourly. Who'd want to come willin·rly to the sorry place?

There were seven men in the barroom, grouped around the only table, silently scanning Bishop. Meeting the cold impact of his return stare, one by one they turned their heads away. Five of them, seated, watched a youthful redhead finish performing a card trick. Their blank faces refused to show the slightest sign of entertainment, but the young sleight-of-hand artist began another trick, smiling, giving the impression of deliberately challenging a hostile audience.

The seventh man of the group stood looking on, bared arms folded, motionless as a statue; a statue gone wrong in the making. He had the enormous torso of a giant, but nature had cheated him. His thick legs were incongruously short, half the length of a grown man's. His bald head was a mass of scars. He wore a soiled shirt unbuttoned wide as if to display his hairy chest. The hair there was as thick as a bear's pelt.

Bishop moved on to the bar, which consisted of plain boards resting on trestles. Presently, taking his time, the bald man stumped around behind it. Without uttering a word, he dribbled whisky sparingly into a chipped and smeary shot-glass, then placed his hand on the bar to indicate his desire for immediate payment. Whisky was apparently all he served. The board sagged under the weight of his hand. He put Bishop's dollar into his pants pocket and produced a half-dollar in change. Bishop left it on the bar.

Even for a full shot of good whisky, fifty cents was a fairly steep price. What Bishop swallowed seemed compounded of red pepper and coal oil, flavored with gunpowder. He looked at the bottle. No label. The bald man, taking his look at the bottle to mean a refill, did the dubious honors while picking up the half-dollar, still without a word. An openhanded son of the West, him, full of genial hospitality.

Bishop grew irritated. Poverty didn't excuse the rude discourtesy of denying a customer the right to pour his own drinks and pay his tote when finished. It would have counted as an insult in the poorest Mexican *cantina.*

The group at the table had meanwhile been casting sly looks in his direction, measuring him up for cash possibilities. One of them finally called to him, "We're gettin' up a game o' stud. Care to sit in?" Dropping his elaborate casualness, the speaker stuck a finger at the young redhead. "Not you!"

Bishop pulled up a broken-backed chair and stacked a few dollars before him. The game turned out to be a niggling matter of dimes and quarters, though the five down-at-heel cowmen played as if for double-eagles. They were amateurs bucking a professional. The grubby cards were marked on the thumbnail system. Bishop crossed them up with some judicious thumbnailing of his own as the cards passed through his hands.

Within minutes he raked in the last pot of chicken feed and rose to his feet. "Where can I buy grain for my horse?" he inquired.

Not responding, the five losers sat sullenly regarding the scattered cards on the table, knowing belatedly they had been flimflammed at their own game. The bald man waddled his gross bulk to the rear, disappeared, and returned carrying a battered tin pail. He spoke for the first time.

"Four dollars."

Bishop inspected the pail. It was less than quarter filled. "Four dollars for that dab?"

"Grain's scarce round here."

"Must be, from the looks of those half-starved nags out front."

The five men raised their heads. The bald man made to take the pail back. Bishop jerked it from him, paid the four dollars, and left. It was a petty penalty imposed on him, a stranger, for winning from regular customers. Well, if charging him four dollars for a dime's worth of grain made them feel any better, they were welcome.

The young redhead came out of the dingy saloon, blinking in the sunshine. Bishop stood by the black while it nosed into the tin pail.

"Could you spare me a little of that grain?"

"No," Bishop grunted, slightly infected by the ill manners of Dry Spring.

"I can pay for it."

"Then why didn't you buy it in there, like I did?"

"Guess I started off on the wrong foot. Like you, I made a remark about their nags. It got their backs up. I've been here a week."

"Hope you're enjoying it," said Bishop.

The redhead grinned wryly. "Not much! These folks are mighty proddy. They scrape out a hardscrabble living. Work a little, steal a little. It's natural they despise strangers. And there's a deputy county sheriff here who's got his eye on me. Guess he figures I'm bound to get in trouble, I stay long enough."

He paused, watching the black deplete the grain. "I had to stop here on account of my horse went lame. He's okay now, only needs strengthening. But these folks won't sell me grain. They've got a down on me. And they know I've got money. Not much. but some. I've been laying out nights in the brush. That's my horse there, the grulla."

Bishop relented a notch. "You can have what grain my horse leaves, if any."

"Thanks, Ro—" The redhead checked himself, changing it to, "Thanks, Mr. Bishop."

"You appear to know me. I don't know you, far's I recall."

"I saw you once in Tucson, a year ago."

"H'mm." Bishop harked back. Ah, yes. That brief affair outside the Shoo-Fly. The Mobley brothers. Didn't

26

seem that long ago, a year. He hadn't been to Tucson since, and wouldn't until that affair blew over.

Sometimes, in rare introspective moments, it occurred to him that he had dug deep tracks in too many places. As a free-lance troubleshooter and gambler, he had to pay vigilant heed to the danger of recrossing his tracks. The hazards increased the longer he lived.

Still, he couldn't imagine himself ever settling down to a humdrum existence. Not even if circumstances permitted him to do so. Which, all things considered, wasn't the remotest bit likely.

Shamrock, her face downcast, said bitterly to Bishop, "Here's your money back. All I could find in this miserable hole was a few yards of dress goods in the so-called general store." She held up a paper-wrapped package. "Shoddy stuff! It's been on the shelf, I bet, since grandma was a bride. And the man had the cussed gall to charge me—"

"Never mind, cool off," Bishop bade her. "Keep the money. Maybe you can do better in Union Junction when we get there. Why did you buy the stuff?"

"Thought I might sort of drape it round me. Look more decent for you. More like a girl." Flushing pink, she dragged off her hat—her father's slouch hat—and fanned herself with it. Her thick dark hair cascaded down in unruly waves. "Phew, it's hot!"

The young redhead perked up, saying, "You sure look like a girl to me!" He doffed his hat to her.

She eyed him stonily. "Who're you to say?"

"My name's Mackenzie. Red Mackenzie. I've been called Red so long I nigh forget my given name," he said chattily. "Matter of fact, me being Scottish from way back, it happens to be—"

"Don't bother," she cut him off. "Keep your hat on, kiltie. Younguns get sunstroke easy."

Young men had tried to get cozy with her before, Bishop surmised. Older men, too. The kid had learned how to defend herself from them. And she, Irish, abhorred the Scots. The redhead didn't stand a chance with her.

"Rogue, when do we pull out of here?"

"Sundown."

"It's a long time to wait."

"Patience, kid. The Rurales will be homeward bound by then. They're on U. S. territory."

The black horse raised its head, chomping, eyes lidded half-closed in the satisfaction of a needed meal. At once, Red Mackenzie grabbed the tin pail and rushed it to his grulla.

"Mr. Bishop," he said, "I heard you say Union Junction is your next destination, sir, did I not?" His choice of words, and his slightly exaggerated accent, Scottish, were remindful of Captain O'Terran's charming Irish blarney.

"You did."

"Would you care for company, sir, you and the young miss? My company. I'm a useful chap, able to—"

"No," said Bishop. And Shamrock, shaking her head, sent him a gratefully approving glance. No third party in their flight. Just the two of them. Together, always.

Bishop's refusal, however, stemmed from the troublesome fact that he already had one sprout on his hands. Damned if he'd encumber himself with another. Red Mackenzie, while not exactly a sprout, hadn't yet attained full manhood. He was at a reckless age that took no thought of consequences. Furthermore, he had a warm eye for Shamrock, which threatened complications that Bishop didn't care to handle. The redhead probably mistook Shamrock as an older girl, more his own age, because of her shapely build, her ripening femaleness that no man could help sensing.

And that, her femaleness, which Bishop had scarcely

28

recognized previously, posed more than enough complications for the future. Awkward complications. A female companion was all very well, but she was so young, hardly more than a child.

It just wouldn't do. So he'd have to pass her off as his daughter, and treat her as such. Be stern to her. Use harshness to discourage affection. And all the while guard her from the skirt-chasers, a full-time occupation, women being so scarce in this country and the men so hungrily virile.

If the tyke had stayed a tomboy . . . How did she manage to blossom out suddenly like the desert larkspur after a rain? Even her body seemed more rounded, her breasts fuller, her walk and movements more feminine. She was going to need considerable guarding, a mighty lot of it as time went by.

Why in hell had he stepped into such a damfool jackpot? Common charity was the only answer. Damn charity! He had always mistrusted it.

# IV

The bald man emerged from the saloon, the five cow-men trailing out behind him. A sweeping look at their faces, their eyes especially, told Bishop they planned mischief.

He sighed, wishing he hadn't skinned the five. Their measly losses rankled. They thought themselves hotshots. Nightfall was hours off, and to buy time until then he was willing to give them back their chicken feed, but the offer would insult them and demean him. He watched the five line up abreast, their maneuver intentionally menacing, aimed at overawing him. They were out to make him crawl. To restore their mangy self-esteem.

Shambling around to the front of the hitching rack, the bald man drawled, "Fine big horse you got there, mister." He was the key to the rigged-up situation. The trigger. His huge paw descended urgently on Shamrock's head. He ruffled her hair. "An' a right fetchin' little filly!"

Shamrock promptly slashed him across the face with her parcel of dress goods while kicking his shin. She followed through with a left hook and another, higher, kick.

"Keep your dirty paws off me, you scruffy *animalucho!*"

It didn't surprise Bishop in the least. Nothing she did could any longer surprise him. She possessed the experience and knowledge to make short work of a mauling man thrice her size. That second kick of hers was a crippler. Bishop hoped he could stave off a shoot-out as a result of her wildcat flare-up.

The surprised one was the bald man. An edge of Shamrock's parcel had scraped an eye, her left hook had

30

bunged the other, and her second kick bowed him over. He swung a wide slap at her face.

Red Mackenzie hammered the reaching arm down, clung to it. It shook him off, the bald man lowering his scarred head to butt him. The redhead stroked out his gun and held it short-gripped in a clubbing position, whereupon the five scrub cowmen made countering motions toward their holsters.

"Wup!" snapped Bishop. He held a gun in each hand, produced in a flash. "Snub it off!"

His hope still hinged on staving off a shoot-out, if possible. If Shamrock was satisfied with the damage she had done. If Red Mackenzie checked his violent proclivities on Shamrock's behalf. If the five would-be hotshots used sense.

The bald man wiped his streaming eyes. "A gunslinger!" he exclaimed, and cursed, glaring at Bishop's brace of long-barrelled guns. He raised his voice to a bellow. "Hey deputy! Gunslinger in town!"

The resident deputy sheriff stepped from a doorway, cradling lightly a double-barrelled shotgun at the ready. He bore the rigid stance and squinch-eyed belligerence of a law officer who wasn't to be trifled with. He was known to be death on gunslingers. His fierce efficiency with a shotgun, and murderously overzealous use of it, perhaps accounted for his having been shunted off into this sparsely populated district.

"Drop your guns!" he commanded Bishop. "You, too, young feller! And step out clear, both o' you." Plainly, only the close proximity of the bald man to his victims deterred him temporarily from loosing a spreading load of buckshot. "Quick, now!"

Bishop, disinclined to fall victim to a killer lawman, pitched two shots that ended all hope of peace. One lifted the deputy's hat off while the other spanged between his boots. The deputy, disconcerted, skipped aside a pace. Red Mackenzie fired and hit the shotgun, which exploded its two loads whistling overhead. The five cowmen backed to the wall of the saloon, and the bald man took to earth. Doors banged.

"Town's coming alive. Time for us to move on," said Red Mackenzie matter-of-factly.

He hoisted Shamrock onto one of the horses tied to the hitching rack, freed its reins, tossed them to her. As if she wasn't perfectly able to perform that service for herself. He jumped onto his grulla and whacked both animals with his hat to start them off running, and off they went.

For Bishop's welfare he showed no regard. His concern lay wholly with the girl, to the desired outcome of having her to himself. To shelter from hardship and peril. To cherish . . .

Bishop overhauled him on the western road, riding alone, Shamrock a speck in the distance.

"Couldn't keep up with her, eh?"

"What's it look like?" Red Mackenzie retorted grumpily "That horse I put her on, it's one of those scrawny-looking crowbaits that'll outrun most anything till its legs give out. The last she said to me, she said, 'Tell Rogue when you see him to hurry up!' "

"I'll do that. Dry Spring is hot after us."

"Well, we did fire on the deputy and steal a horse."

"Right," Bishop agreed, not troubling to argue about who stole the horse. "Three or four ranches between here and Union Junction, I believe, where you might find cover if you're pressed."

"Uh-huh. Or a faster horse." Red Mackenzie squinted after the speck ahead. "With luck I could join you in Union Junction."

"Don't strain for it. We'll only stop there to pick up an outfit for her. You're not invited."

"Didn't I help—"

"Nobody asked you to horn in. S'long!"

"Wait a minute! What's her name?"

"It's O'Terran, and she doesn't take to Scots," Bishop replied discouragingly. "And I don't like sprigs triggering in on my play. You're on your own, kiltie. Make the best of it."

He caught up with Shamrock. Her skin-and-bones mount flagged woefully, strength spent on its burst of speed. Without grain it lacked endurance, like Red Mackenzie's grulla. The nourishing seeds of grama grass, free feed farther north on open range, didn't exist here in this hungry country.

"Get up behind me."

She dismounted. "Where's the redhead?" she inquired.

He waited while she threw off the saddle and turned loose the drooping pony. A humane act. "He's back there riding rearguard," he said, eyes on her face, watching for her reaction.

She shrugged indifferently. "Rearguard, hell! That grulla of his is a goat!" She sprang up behind Bishop on the powerful big black. "We don't need him. We don't need anybody . . ."

Union Junction, a crossroads town supported largely by two struggling stagelines, north-south and east-west, and by a freightline that operated whenever there was paying freight to haul and the driver could be found sober, had an edge on Dry Spring. Not a great edge, but sufficient to inspire sniffs of superiority.

For one thing, it had a fairly good saloon.

The saloon, owned on shares by leading townsmen, was run by a clean Englishman who had the benevolent manners of a butler and the capable fists of a thug. Besides tending bar, he kept an eye on the poker tables and collected a tithe from every pot, supposedly for the house. God help any winner trying to hold out on him. He could slug cruelly faster than a man could draw a gun or knife. Common knowledge had it that he had reached the United States via Australia. An escapee from the penal colonies for criminals.

"See your five, raise ten," Bishop said, bluffing, and made it.

He raked in the pot. He extracted three dollars from it for the tithe and laid them aside. The watchful subject of Victoria Regina sent him a courtly nod of gracious appreciation from behind the bar, wishing that all his customers were such freehanded gentlemen. Some of the stageline passengers, stopping overnight, were sticky jaspers. And the locals on the whole were cheap.

The deal came to Bishop. A player dropped out and another took his chair. Shuffling the deck, giving the cut, he raised his eyes to the newcomer and looked into the freckled young face of Red Mackenzie.

"You again!" he grunted, deciding immediately to skin him down to his socks and send him adrift. He flipped the cards out. The game was draw poker, no cards wild.

"Me again," the redhead said cheerfully. "Must be fate. Where's the young lady?"

"Miss O'Terran," said Bishop, "is out buying clothes for herself. If they can be bought here. Which I doubt."

"Your pardon, sir, I call a fault on the deal. You dealt me a card from the bottom of the deck."

Wordlessly, Bishop gathered up the cards and sat fully prepared for developments. The rest of the players shoved their chairs back. The redhead grinned at him, his hands spread apart on the table.

"It was an accidental slip of your finger, I don't doubt. No hard feelings, sir. I've done the same."

"I pass the deal to you," Bishop said, "if nobody objects. Maybe you'll do better."

"I can try."

There were no objections, because the rest of the players quit, leaving the tussle to the two of them. Two sharks. A seasoned gambler against a sharp-eyed youth. It promised shattering results. Onlookers, crowding around the table, muttered under-breath, pulling for the youth.

While Red Mackenzie still shuffled the pack, Shamrock entered the saloon, still dressed in canvas pants and faded flannel shirt, wearing her dead father's heavy six-shooter and shell-studded gunbelt. An armed urchin. Sweeping a searching look over the barroom, she located Bishop and darted behind him.

"Rogue, that deputy sheriff's in town with a posse!" she hissed into his ear. "I think they saw me before I could duck out of sight, but they stopped at the marshal's office. I took your horse from the livery. It's out back."

Bishop came to his feet. "Sorry, got to go," he told Red Mackenzie.

"Trouble?"

"Dry Spring law. Look after yourself."

"Heigh-ho! And me with a borrowed-without-leave buckskin in the street!"

"That's your problem."

" 'Deed it is!"

Going to the bar, and unobtrusively laying a twenty on it, Bishop said to the Englishman, "A rear exit, please, and a closed mouth for five minutes."

"Right this way," responded the Englishman, asking no questions. He lifted the bar-flap, bowing Bishop and Shamrock through. "I regret the loss of your patronage so soon. To me it has been most enjoyable, educational, and, I may's well say, profitable."

"You run a nice place."

"Thank you. All mouths will be closed, I guarantee."

They passed through a storeroom and on through small

but tidy living quarters, to a bolted rear door. Back in the barroom, someone entered on heavy feet, followed by the tread of several others. A voice rapped, "Who here rode in on the buckskin out front? It's a stolen horse!"

"That's our town marshal," the Englishman said, drawing the bolts of the door. "Not a bad sort of chap, though stupid. I presume he means the young Scot."

"Correct."

Shamrock turned from the opened door. "Let's give that kiltie a hand, Rogue!"

"Not on your life!" Bishop caught hold of her and marched her out. "I give the orders. Bear it in mind."

She struggled, furiously indignant, forcing him to lift her off her feet. "You're a hard-nosed, merciless bastard!"

"And you're an unholy terror!"

While closing the rear door after them, the Englishman promised, "I'll do what I can for the lad. Goodnight, and happy journeying to you both." Bolting the door, he wagged his head. An outstanding pair of hellions, those two. Born to trouble.

Gaining the westward stageroad after skirting wide out of Union Junction, with Shamrock up behind him again on the black, Bishop decided definitely that he must get rid of her. The sooner the better.

She was a marker, like a red filly in a stolen band of dun horses. Anywhere he might go, as long as she was along with him, she marked him for the searching law: notorious longrider with a young girl in tow.

And she was a spitfire, impulsive. Difficult to manage. Rebellious, headstrong. A savage. Her father hadn't imposed the least bit of discipline on her, the ordinary discipline that a youngster needed and unconsciously wanted, to give her a sense of security, of belonging in a real and regulated way of life.

Probably it was too late now to attempt to arouse

that sense in her. She was far gone in lawlessness. The outlaw stamp badged her for anyone to see. It emblazoned her actions and strong speech.

Paying deep thought to the puzzle, Bishop hit on a possible solution. Or, at any rate, a stopgap. A release from bondage. It was up to the sprat to make the most of it, if she had the makings.

Her outburst of temper spent, she leaned against him, contrite and remorseful, rubbing her cheek on the back of his coat, too yieldingly affectionate for his peace of mind. "Where do we go now?"

"To a town where an old friend of mine lives. Real nice town, quiet, where you can't get into any mischief if you tried. It's called Piety, matter of fact."

She stiffened. "Why go there?" She stopped rubbing her cheek on his coat. "I don't even like the name of it!"

The tide of Bishop's charity ebbed lower. "We're going to Piety because I say so!" he snapped, heeling the black horse onward, hurryingly anxious to put an end to his dilemma.

"Is your Piety friend a woman?"

"A lady."

"Whoo! Sometimes I could kill you!"

"Don't try. I'll lay you over my knee and whack hell out of you!"

Belatedly, he realized that it was the wrong thing for him to say. She wriggled, snuggling against him, secure in the knowledge that he could care enough to wallop her should the need arise.

"I bet you would, you big hound!" Then, after a minute or two: "Is your lady-friend pretty?"

"I didn't say she's a lady-friend. Just a friend. I knew her when she owned a business in Tombstone."

Shamrock tightened her arms around him. "If she's

not a lady-friend of yours," she asked with forthright practicality, "what are you going to her for?"

"To see if she'll take you in, give you a decent home," Bishop said. *And get you off my neck*, he could have added. "Behave yourself when you meet her."

"But I don't want a home! What's wrong with going on the way we are?"

"Everything!"

# V

Bishop rattled his fingernails on the front door of the big white house. He stepped back into the moon-shadow of a massive porch column. He didn't have to tell Shamrock to do the same; she knew well how to melt into convenient shadows when in territory that was unfamiliar and therefore potentially hostile. Her right hand rested on the butt of her holstered gun.

"Take it easy, girl! This town's safe."

"Then what are we hiding for? Why did you hide the horse under the cottonwoods?"

Stumped for an adequate and believable explanation, he shrugged, saying simply, "Common caution." But common caution didn't cover it, not by far. His sense of danger prickled, as if eyes watched him in the dark.

The big white house stood at the southern end of the main street, near the creek and the cottonwoods. It had an air of having been pinned onto the town as an ornament, never becoming an integral part of it. Its whiteness was too white, its scrimshaw scrollwork too lavish. The rounded fanlights over the tall windows were paned with expensive colored glass. The front columns were a Southern planter's dream, pre-Civil War.

"She'll welcome us, girl, don't you worry."

While awaiting the welcome, Bishop surveyed what he could see of this town of Piety in the dark. He had visited here before, briefly. He remembered distinctly the odd location of the sheriff's office and the jail, built flush alongside the bank, the jail on the second floor with a porticoed walk around it. The Keller Bank; yes, of course. Midway on the Keller Block, across the wide street from the Bearcat Saloon. The Bearcat. Queer name for a saloon deep in the Southwest. In a wild town the name would slyly imply a different meaning: Bare Cat. But not here.

A respectable town, this, loaded with prosperity and civic pride. Its solid citizens were mostly mine owners and cattle ranchers able to afford a house in town, and businessmen. Some fine residences stood proudly back there among the scattered lights.

It was a civilized town, orderly, law-abiding. An air of Puritan rectitude positively pervaded it. It had been founded and named by a party of earnest Mormons, now long gone. A healthful place in which to raise a family. On Sunday morning you could walk sedately to the Baptist church, listen to the piping song of meadowlarks in the blazing sun, and detect from their thoughtful demeanor those of the prominent male townsmen who got trimmed last night at the Bearcat's poker tables; or in the expensively private little rooms of the hotel above.

Bishop didn't personally care for the town. His tastes ran to a faster tempo, to places where a broadminded tolerance of human foibles and misdoings prevailed. Roaring goldcamps and wide-open trailtowns, for first choice. However, he could concede that Piety had excellent points to recommend it to people who preferred a safely substantial existence.

"You'll wear nice dresses here," he murmured encouragingly to Shamrock, "and be a real lady. Maybe go to school." He moved to the door and tapped on it again. And again his sense of danger prickled. Yet this dark end of the street showed no movement.

Shamrock kept her thoughts to herself. The Captain had not neglected her schooling. Camps had been classrooms, and the curriculum included lessons in subjects that were not usually studied by a young girl.

The door of the big white house swung inward. A

woman stepped forth, blonde and statuesque, the light behind her in the hall outlining her so that she appeared like a golden goddess in a stage play, making her grand entrance on stage. Her conscious stateliness at the same time hinted of defiance, angry defiance.

She had donned a long cape of sapphire-blue velvet against the cool night air, a gorgeously rich raiment that hid her arms and hands. "Who knocked on my door?" she demanded of the night.

Her voice was a husky contralto. She stared about at the outside darkness.

"Show yourselves, or I look for you with a sawed-off shotgun!" She produced the weapon from beneath the cape, both of its rabbit-eared hammers cocked over twin barrels that were cut short to twelve inches.

Bishop smiled, pleased to observe that her retirement from a full and active life hadn't seemed as yet to have dulled her forthrightness. "Tie up your wolf, Bonny!" he said, stepping into the light.

At the sound of his gravelly voice and the sight of his large figure, she raised the sawed-off shotgun skyward and eased down the hammers. She opened wide her fine blue eyes. Her generous mouth opened, too, in a dazzling smile of heartfelt welcome.

"Well! If it isn't—" she began, and cut herself off, sweeping a distrustful look at the surrounding darkness. "Come in," she whispered. "Are they crowding you, Rogue?"

"A little," Bishop said. "But that's not why I'm calling on you. It's something else. Something you'll cuss me for. I won't blame you."

"Quit the yammering and come in!"

"Come on, Shamrock."

They slipped inside, a couple of tired wanteds, seeking food and rest. And across the street a man, the town drunk, hitherto motionless in shadow, got up and headed upstreet for the Keller Block and the sheriff's office. There surely was a cash bounty posted for that big devil . . .

"Shamrock, meet Miss Blue. Bonny, this is Miss Shamrock O'Terran."

Bishop performed the introduction gravely, inwardly amused.

They stood in the drawing room, a large chamber of rather overwhelming magnificence. The massive furniture, gilt-framed pictures, heavy draperies and thick rugs reminded Bishop of the plushy gambling palace that Bonny Belle Blue had owned and operated in Tombstone for several profitable years. In fact, he thought he recognized some of the pieces.

Bonny Belle didn't blink an eyelash as she took the hand of the ragged urchin. "Charmed," she purred graciously. "I'm sure you want to wash up, change into comfortable attire, and rest yourself. Let me show you to a guestroom, my dear . . ."

In suitable environment she could act the grand lady, a perfect hostess. Occasionally a rough edge of her past life obtruded.

When she returned alone to the drawing room, she eyed Bishop searchingly. "Huh!" she snorted. "I've known you to tangle in one or two mad doings, and heard tell of a lot more. All right, you're a lobo. You trouble-shoot for profit. That's understood. But this throws me! Where did you pick up that poor kid? It's not like you, Rogue, to take—"

"Not like me," Bishop agreed, "so drop it. She's still a virgin. D'you like her?"

He had discovered and explored the liquor-and-wine sideboard during her absence. He poured two brandies from a cut-glass decanter and handed her one.

"Too soon to tell." Bonny Belle raised her glass to

him and drank it empty. "After she's washed and gets into some decent clothes—"

"Tried buying clothes for her along the way, but things happened. We were hurrying. It got a mite hot for us, here and there." Bishop refilled Bonny's outstretched glass.

He noticed that her hand trembled slightly. "You've put on a little weight since I saw you last," he said a bit cruelly.

"Nice of you to mention it!" she retorted, aiming a freezing glance at him over her lifted brandy glass. She was still quite young enough to be vain of her voluptuous figure.

"And your color's not what it was."

"Any other compliments?"

"You're drinking too much. The signs are showing."

She started to call him a liar, but refrained, knowing he spoke the truth. "You make it hard for a lady to keep in mind she's a lady," she told him.

It was because of her aspirations to gentility that she had sold her gambling palace, quit rowdy Tombstone, and moved to respectable Piety. After spending a fortune on the house and its furnishings, she felt qualified to mingle socially with genteel people. She possessed style and polish, and plenty of experience in entertaining company. She waited to receive courtesy calls from the wives of Piety's foremost citizens, prepared to meet them on equal terms, to nurture friendships which would lead to dinner parties and dances.

She still waited, without hope. The wives distrusted her, a single woman, flamboyantly attractive. Fearing for their husbands, they carefully avoided her. Gossip grew that her money came from darkly nefarious sources. The only callers were tradesmen's delivery boys. Her splendid big house had become a subject for leering speculation among men. Anything connected with it got smeared.

She couldn't keep servants, though paying them generously.

Loneliness bred boredom. Boredom led to brandy. Bishop could trace the route, not surprised at it. Bonny Belle Blue, despite all her experience, retained a naive innocence underneath the brittle exterior. She was a patsy for anyone with elegant manners.

"Now I'll tell you about Shamrock," Bishop said. And he did, crisply, leaving out nothing of importance except that the girl was utterly impossible to manage.

Bonny Belle eyed him shrewdly when he finished. "A sprig from a poison oak! I've heard of mad Captain O'-Terran and his fighty brat. Why did you bring her here?"

Bishop twirled his glass. "Got any cigars? I'm out."

"The silver box, there on the sideboard. 'Fraid they're stale by this time."

He selected a cigar, crunched the end off, lit it. "On the dry side, but good tobacco. The Cubans know how to make a good smoke. Can't beat Havana cigars."

"Answer my question, will you? Why did you bring O'Terran's brat here?"

"Oh, that. Sure." He inhaled, puffed. "Bonny, did I ever do you a favor?"

"Yes, a couple times. What d'you want?"

He set down the glass and cigar, and met her straight stare. "Take her off my hands! Take her in and give her a home! She's got good blood in her. Wild, I grant. Wild as a hawk. Like her father. He wasn't any angel, God knows, but he was pretty much of a man."

"So they say."

"If you won't take her in, I'll have to turn her adrift and let her shift for herself."

"Rogue, you wouldn't! Not you."

"She'll get me killed if I don't! Then what becomes of her? They'll put her in a foster home. The kitchen drudge. A cot in the barn. Wearing cast-offs. And the hired men—"

"Oh, shut up!" Bonny Belle wrinkled her nose at him. "You win. I'll take her in. This damn' house won't be so ungodly empty, with a youngster in it."

"*Bueno!*" Bishop breathed.

A vast relief and a sense of liberty brought to his hard mouth a smile that was real and rare. His final card, the threat to set the girl adrift, was a bluff and Bonny Belle probably knew it, but it had turned the trick. Once more he was on his own, nobody but himself to worry about. No burdensome encumbrance.

Yet he felt a small twinge of loss, an odd reluctance to cut the girl entirely out of his life, causing him to say, "If it doesn't work, Bonny, write to me."

"Where? Where do you ever stay long enough for mail to catch up with you?"

"Care of the Wells Fargo station at Wickenburg. I know the agent. He'll hold it for me to pick up, or forward it on. I'll get here. May take time. Hello, Shamrock," he said as the girl sped into the room. "Thought you were in bed. What's your rush?"

Bathed and scrubbed to a pink glow, wearing a frilly nightgown that trailed too long and large for her, Shamrock darted around dimming the lights of the ornate brass lanps.

"*Cuidado!*"

Bishop shot to his feet, recalling the sense of danger that had prickled him before entering the house. "What's up?"

"Men outside on watch!" she replied tersely. "Somebody saw us come in. I *knew* I smelled skunk! So did you."

"I did," Bishop agreed. But he hadn't believed that the tendrils of law had reached this far so soon. Besides, never had he done Piety any harm. "You're sure?"

"Spotted them from an upstairs window. They're hunkered behind bushes in the front yard, waiting. You wait for me, Rogue! We'll gun it out of here!" Shamrock's bare feet pattered off.

Bishop whirled swiftly. "Go after her, Bonny! She's gone for her gun. Hold her back. I'm going. Good luck!"

"Same to you," Bonny Belle returned. She had known men who died a violent death. Reckless men. Friends. God, how many? Lying face-down in a dusty street. Or bushwhacked in the hills. Or word trickled from way below the border that he had backed the wrong general. An adobe wall and a firing squad.

"You need good luck more'n I do, Rogue."

"I'm not so sure about that. I can bust these two-bit town warriors. You've got Shamrock to handle."

She stood tensely listening after he left the drawing room, knowing better than to follow him into the hallway. No sound reached her of the front door's opening and closing. She thought he must still be in the house.

Voices suddenly rang out in challenging query. At once, a stuttering blare of exploding cartridges gave answer. Bonny Belle Blue rolled her eyes upward. If she had stood any slightest chance of ever becoming accepted by Piety, this queered it.

She heard men go scrambling around the house, swearing, blundering into one another in their rush to take cover from that shatteringly fast barrage. Then presently the beat of a ridden horse, fading off, and shocked silence.

The soberly sedate town of Piety would not soon forget this night, not forgive her for it. There would be harsh questions, severe accusations of harboring a wanted man. She'd have to claim in defense that he forced himself into her home. And Shamrock? Well, he had this kid he'd picked up, and he dropped her off . . .

Somebody outside called, "What in hell *was* it? A shooting tornado?"

"We'll ask the woman!" said the sheriff grimly. "Anybody get a shot at him?"

"You kidding? Here he came an' there he went! Streak o' black lightning. I hit earth. Man, his guns!"

Shamrock came flying into the drawing room, the frilly nightgown stuffed into her grimed canvas pants, gunbelt strapped on, the gun in her hand.

"Has he gone off and left me here?" she blazed. Tears and wrath glistened her eyes. "The double-crossing hound! I don't want to be a lady, dammit, I want to be with him!"

"He's gone, kid," Bonny Belle said, listening for the sheriff's knock on the front door. "He had to go. You're stuck with me. And," she muttered, "I'm stuck with you, God help us!"

# VI

Piety didn't forget or forgive the outrage that had been committed against its civic orderliness. For a while, some pressure was put on the sheriff to take legal action, especially by the women. They wanted *That Woman* run out of town. Her past was notorious. Her grand house offended them.

The harried sheriff protested that he couldn't properly charge the woman with anything. A gunslinger had forced his way into her house and planted a stray waif in her hands. That was her story; try cracking it. The sheriff had tried hard, and got nowhere, defeated by Bonny Belle Blue's pseudo-innocent gaze and lofty words.

Frustrated, the townspeople talked about the woman and the girl in the big white house. Particularly the girl, Shamrock O'Terran. The fact seeped out that she was the daughter of the raffishly disreputable Captain O'Terran. Wild blood. Born to trouble.

As time passed, confident prediction turned to irritation. The girl did nothing to justify any suspicion. She had no fear of venturing forth and doing the shopping, keeping an eye on Bonny's bills, quickly detecting overchargings. The tradesmen learned to respect her, and they stopped padding the account.

In her behavior she was more circumspect than half of the local girls. Virile cowboys fresh in off the range, meeting her coolly amused look, went searching afield further for more possible game.

Feeling that she was spitefully cheating them, people watched her all the closer. They watched the big white house that was supposedly a mysterious pit of hidden

sin ruled over by *That Woman*, Bonny Belle Blue. They
watched with hope and ready condemnation, not knowing what it was they expected, but sure that the erup-
tion would have its start in Shamrock O'Terran. They
watched her grow from a harum-scarum urchin into a
self-possessed young lady of nineteen, and they didn't
relent.

She was a strange one. Vivid as a Spanish shawl, she
went quietly about her business, seemingly oblivious of
the effect she created. Or simply not caring. She bore an
impenetrable wall of reserve, of stoical remoteness from
her surroundings, in the way that a potentially dangerous captive might cloak impatience—or the patient, boil-
ing-beneath waiting for a break-out.

When she walked through the town, all eyes followed
her lithe, springy stride. The people of Piety sensed that
here was something wild and elemental, a force held
in leash, beyond the grubby understanding of town-tame
citizens. A disturbing creature of hidden fire. Women
curled their lips at her. Men licked theirs.

None of them knew a thing of what she thought of
them, except that she was able to mock and flay brash
men with only a glance from her dark, scornful eyes.
Dark blue. Her eyes actually were blue, but so deeply
blue as to appear almost black when she lowered her
long lashes. Whenever a gust of wind swirled in off the
desert, catching her outdoors, she stood as if listening
to a distant voice.

She invariably slowed her step, passing the end of the
Keller Block where the sheriff's office adjoined the Keller
Bank. Her pause paid tribute to a faded and yellowed bill
pasted on the sheriff's wanted board. The bill named
Rogue Bishop and gave a sketchy description of him. It
represented a link to former years, a nostalgic reminder
of a far different life.

Mansell Keller, Jr., usually took the opportunity to

come to the door of the bank when Shamrock paused, and would bow and speak polite greetings to her. His courteous advances, each time more pressing, miffed people who believed that the son and heir of Piety's most prominent citizen should be more discreet, certainly more discriminating. There were *nice* girls for him to choose from, locally raised girls.

Old traditions, sighed the diehards, were sadly crumbling. The Bearcat Saloon had grown noisy with an influx of gun-slung newcomers, and the sheriff did nothing about it. There were rumors of trouble out on the range, settlers and small cattlemen strangely quitting, close-mouthed, leaving for parts unknown. In Piety itself, long-held properties were changing ownership.

The town wasn't what it used to be, since the coming of *That Woman*. Blame it on her.

Bonny Belle, with empty time to spare, had formed the habit of observing trifles and connecting them in her mind, arriving at conclusions that weren't always accurate. Having made no headway with the people of Piety, she concentrated all of her attention on Shamrock. They had developed a steadfast affection for each other; two souls sharing an ostracized existence.

"Do you like him?" she asked, meaning young Mansell Keller. "I've noticed how you always stop by there."

"He's an ornery hound," Shamrock answered absently, meaning Rogue Bishop. "Sure I like him. Always will."

That struck Bonny Belle as a queer way to put it. She hadn't perceived anything ornery or particularly houndish about the banker's son. Kind of a handsome young duck, if your fancy ran to a neat moustache and glossy hair, but not terribly forceful. Not the type she would have expected Shamrock to care for. Well, you never knew . . .

Lying awake in her bed that night, Bonny Belle gave thought to it. She didn't sleep well any more, even with the help of brandy. As soon as she put out the light and slipped into bed, a sensation of imprisonment crept over her. She had mad impulses to run singing through the town, dance in the street—anything for action.

Then her heart would start acting up again, thumping and palpitating. It worried her. Broken sleep brought a recurrent nightmare of walls closing in and smothering her, from which she awoke gasping for air.

The wakeful hours induced long thoughts. So Shamrock had her eye on Mr. Mansell J. Keller's son, the prize catch of Piety. She was aiming impossibly high.

Yet perhaps not entirely impossible. Young Mansell found her mightily attractive, that was evident. His father dominated him, but he probably had a mind of his own. He had every right to marry the girl of his own choice. If his choice was Shamrock . . .

"Lord!" Bonny Belle whispered in the dark, carried away by the vision. "Mrs. Mansell Keller, Junior! A married lady!"

From the beginning, the night of Bishop's visit, she had set out to make a lady of Shamrock. She wasn't at all sure whether she'd had much success so far. The town definitely didn't think so, and never would unless Shamrock married into a good family. Acceptance, no matter how unwilling, would follow.

Mrs. Mansell Keller, Jr. A star of Piety society.

Bonne Belle recalled her own lost ambitions and bright daydreams. She had failed for herself, but maybe a miracle lay in store for Shamrock.

"Count me on your side, kid!" she whispered. "I'll do all I can to help."

She dozed off. The smothering walls for once didn't close in on her that night.

Next day she went to old Dr. Pennyfeather for an examination, squaring up to the fact that something was seriously wrong with her. There was a younger doctor whose looks she liked better, but he had fractured a leg and collarbone in a buggy upset.

Dr. Pennyfeather cupped a hand behind his good ear and listened to Bonny Belle's description of her troublesome symptoms. He was an institution in Piety. Aged residents swore by him, claiming he was so capable he hadn't had to read any medical books in fifty years.

"Hum—bad," he mumbled.

He listened to her heart for a long time, working his shaggy brows portentously, which made her nervous. She felt her heart palpitate. "Very bad, Miss—hum—Blue."

He thoroughly disapproved of her, the more so since he detected a distinct aroma of brandy. He belonged to a temperance society and an anti-gambling league, and had taken a leading part in the attempt to have her run out of town.

"I'll give you some pills that should, hum, depress the action of your heart and help you sleep. That's all."

"Meaning you can't cure me?" she asked him.

He took that as an affront to his vast skill. "When a heart gets into the condition yours is in," he stated severely, "no doctor on earth can cure it!"

"You sound awful positive."

"I am!" A look of bleak triumph in his nearsighted eyes spelled that the wages of sin was death and very rightly so. "Take one of these pills at night. No more than one."

Bonny Belle returned home, facing the verdict that she wasn't likely to live long. It decided her on the pressing necessity to make plans for Shamrock's future; and, furthermore, to put the plans into operation.

She sallied to battle wearing fine attire and a dazzling smile, and stormed the private sanctum of Mr. Mansell J. Keller. Now that her restless spirit had an outlet, a concrete problem for her to grapple with, the vista of a short life ahead couldn't conquer her.

Mr. Mansell J. Keller, known respectfully as the Senior, received Bonny Belle into his office with the coolly impersonal courtesy he reserved for would-be borrowers whose collateral he knew to be shaky. She kept only a modest account in his bank, for convenience.

It had quickly reached his ears that she was under the doctor's care. He surmised that her financial affairs were in bad shape, like her health. She probably wanted to raise a loan on her house, to tide her through. That white elephant. A flat no. He'd risk no money on that.

Besides the bank and the Keller Block, he owned or held controlling interest in various businesses. He was acquiring ranch properties. The Keller name was gaining attention throughout the Territory. Its rising prestige wasn't built on poor risks like loans to dying women.

"I need your advice," Bonny Belle opened, seating herself gracefully in the chair he motioned her to beside his desk. "Advice on how to invest my money." Her innocent eyes let him understand that she was a helpless woman appealing to a tower of male strength and limitless wisdom.

The Senior thawed visibly, paying her a new interest, personal and professional. Bonny Belle contratulated herself. Dangle the right bait, stand-offish men quit being frozen fish and grew human. She still had the stuff. Keller was a widower.

"Your money, Miss Blue? You don't have very much on deposit here."

"No, it's in a Tombstone bank. I write checks on it when my account here runs low. Your cashier handles them."

"Spending your capital, eh? Very foolish."

"I guess it is. That's why I've come to you." She fluttered her fingers. "I don't know anything about business."

"That I can believe! Can you give me a rough idea of your present finances?"

She could and did. The Senior raised his eyebrows, impressed. His courtesy increased. He came around behind her chair and placed his hands on her shoulders. "My dear lady, you do need advice and guidance, don't you?"

"Oh, I do." She had never before needed any. But never before had she campaigned to get a girl wedded.

"I suggest you invest in mortgages. Safe and sound mortgages, carefully chosen, will bring you a good income without depleting your assets."

"How would I—"

"This bank is at your service. We'll attend to all the details. Leave everything in our hands. We have experience in appraising investment opportunities."

"You are most kind, Mr. Keller."

"My pleasure, Miss Blue. You might write your check now, if you wish."

Bonny Belle wrote the check. "I've made my will," she mentioned, "Leaving everything I own to Shamrock. I don't have any kin that I know of. She's like a young sister to me. Or a daughter, nearly."

"You're not old enough to have a grown daughter," said the Senior gallantly, picking up the check. "Isn't she an orphan?"

"So am I," said Bonny Belle a bit sharply. She had been a foundling. Her name she had cooked up when leaving the orphanage at fourteen.

"I'm sorry," he murmured.

She recovered her soft charm. "Shamrock doesn't understand business any better than I do. Could you drop by the house and explain mortgages to her? But I'm afraid that's asking too—"

"Gladly, dear lady! Gladly!" The Senior snapped his fingers. "No, let's make it dinner at my house. This evening? Good! My son will call for you and your lovely ward."

Like that. Success beyond dream.

Bonny Belle entered her house in a golden haze of glory, calling to Shamrock, "I've done it! I put it over!"

"You don't have to yell, Bonny," Shamrock said, emerging from the kitchen, flour up to her elbows. "What's the celebration?"

"We're invited to dine with the Kellers tonight! The Kellers, in the Keller house! Upper crust! The top! And the Senior himself is going to invest my money for me! How d'you like that, eh? How d'you like it?"

Shamrock didn't say how she liked it. Thoughtfully, she inquired if Bonny had anything to show for her money.

Bubbling, Bonny brushed off the question. "Fix yourself up, lovey. Your best dress. Mind you do your hair nice, piled up. Wear my pearl earrings . . ."

Dinner at the Keller house was a success. Bonny Belle wore a shimmering satin gown under her sapphire-blue velvet cloak, and drew warm compliments from the Senior. Young Mansell poured attention on Shamrock. Afterward, it occurred to Bonny that Shamrock had hardly spoken during the evening. Natural, she supposed. Her first dinner party. It was difficult, though, to imagine her as a shy girl.

Other little social occasions followed, a share of them instigated by Bonny Belle and held in her house, she presiding as a lively hostess. At none of them was business discussed, nor so much as mentioned. Bonny Belle blossomed. Shamrock maintained her thoughtful reserve.

The town took astonished notice. Tongues wagged.

But the Senior's position raised him above open criticism. His prestige stemmed partly from a general sense of caution that verged on fear, everyone aware that somehow disaster struck those who stood against him. Nobody in Piety dared to snub him or his son. If the Kellers thought fit to accept those two females, that was that. Swallow it and tag along.

"I've broken the ice at last!" Bonny Belle exulted to Shamrock, who smiled at her and said nothing. "We'll be riding high! The upper crust! Bless that Senior. Guess I've made a hit with him."

# VII

The Senior had a different version of the matter. Speaking to his son in a private man-to-man talk, he said, "I've got to go on buttering-up the woman, to keep her from asking me questions about her money."

Stretched out in a chair, Mansell was admiring his new riding boots. He seldom rode a horse, but liked wearing the gear of a horseman. "So that's the reason. Where's her money gone?"

"In the vault. I had her check cashed in Tombstone."

"Then why—"

"Listen! You know I've spread out these last couple of years. There have been heavy expenses. I had to draw on the bank and juggle the books."

"That's a felony, isn't it? Taking depositors' money for your own use?"

The Senior winced, lighting a Havana cigar. "Don't remind me! The bank examiners are due soon, and those fellows you can't bribe or break. That woman's fifty thousand dollars covers the shortage."

"How long can you stall her?" Mansell asked.

"Until she drops dead, I hope! I didn't give her a receipt, but she'll have the canceled check for proof, made out to me and with my signed endorsement on it. I've got to keep that money in the vault. Must have it always there ready on hand for emergencies."

"Emergencies? You're the richest man—"

"On paper, yes. But I'm spread out thin, robbing Peter to pay Paul, so to speak. In a year or less I'll be solidly on top. Meantime, the whole thing could collapse if somebody took me to court. My affairs won't stand any investigation. There'd be charges of criminal actions."

"Those settlers, you mean, and little cattlemen." Mansell forgot his shiny new boots. "They won't talk. Our men do a good job. One night I rode out with Zeigler—"

"There are others who can talk," his father interrupted him. "A good many others. Let me get in a bind, everybody will turn on me. Everybody! They'll crowd to give evidence! They'll lose their fear of me. Cash in the vault is our security."

"If the woman dropped dead tomorrow," Mansell said, "there's Shamrock. She inherits. What if she demands the fifty thousand dollars and goes to court for it? She could!"

"I know that. How are you getting along with her? I haven't seen you making much headway."

"She's very quiet."

"A quiet woman is heaven's rarest gift to a man," said the Senior. "Marry her and keep her quiet!"

"What?" Mansell exclaimed, startled. "She's a damned pretty girl, but marriage wasn't what I—"

"Marry her!" the Senior repeated. "Put her under your thumb, or we may both go to jail!"

Presently, stroking his trim mustache, Mansell shrugged, smiled. "No hardship. She'll be grateful to marry into our family. Considering what she came from, she'll jump at the chance. All right, I'll marry her."

"You have my parental blessing, son. I'll help you make her into a docile and obedient wife."

"Don't worry, I'll keep her quiet."

"We both will!"

The evening Mansell proposed marriage, the moon was full, the air sultry, the time ripe for a maiden to fall into a man's arms and surrender forthwith.

Shamrock O'Terran held her hands tightly locked behind her back, fingers clasped, to keep herself from hitting Mansell for the smugly cocksure manner in which he couched his proposal.

They stood on the front steps of the big white house, to which Mansell had become a persistent visitor of late. Inside the house, windows open, Bonny Belle was playing the piano and singing a love song. Shamrock gazed at the lighted windows, listening to the hearty contralto tones.

Dear, kind, generous Bonny. She was happy these days, full of laughter, a gay and beautiful woman. Men raised their hats to her on the street, and women offered her polite greetings. At last she was winning acceptance by the upper crust of Piety, and glorying in it. It would be dastardly ungrateful to spoil it for her. She deserved to reach the pinnacle of her ambition before she died. Shamrock knew of the doctor's grim verdict: A few months at most, perhaps only weeks.

Shamrock looked critically at Mansell, at his smooth face and neat little mustache. In his off-hours from the bank, where his father had recently promoted him to manager, Mansell liked to wear dashing range attire. A white hat, fringed buckskin vest, high-heeled riding boots polished to a glister. Dude garb that was recognized as false at a glance by any working cowman or range rider.

Maybe she could stand him for a short while, put up with him for Bonny's sake. "Yes, I'll marry you," Shamrock gave her answer matter-of-factly.

Mansell seized her hands in his. "When? Name the day!" He was the fervent lover, pushed in part by the nagging thought of fifty thousand dollars in the bank vault.

"This," said Shamrock shamelessly, "is so sudden. Give me time. Next year?"

"No, no, this year! This month!"

"Cripes!" In for a penny, in for a pound, as the Captain used to say. "Well, all right."

The announcement of the forthcoming marriage rocked Piety. Shamrock wrote a note to Rogue Bishop, addressing it in care of the Wells Fargo agent in Wickenburg for the agent to forward on to wherever Bishop might be at the time. Her note, so formal as to be puckishly ironic, invited Mr. Rogate Bishop to the wedding. She didn't imagine for a minute that Bishop would show up. The faded and yellowed notice still clung to the wall of the sheriff's office, posting him as wanted. In effect, her note was her final farewell to him.

The day of the wedding arrived with such bright cheer it irritated Shamrock. The skies should have been blackly ominous, thunder rolling.

She had refused all help in dressing, and in her bedroom mirror she scowled at her reflection in bridal gown and veil. A church wedding, full scale, all the trimmings; nothing less for the lordly Kellers. She felt a wicked temptation to put on her old canvas pants and flannel shirt and stroll to church in them, just to see the shocked consternation on the faces.

In the plushy drawing room the Senior smiled at a resplendent Bonny Belle Blue. They were alone. He suggested a toast to the happy occasion. Bonny, adequately brandied, waved him cordially to her wine cabinet.

The Senior chose a decanter of sherry from the cabinet, a drink which Bonny held in rather low esteem except as a nightcap. "I saw a small bottle of pills in there," he mentioned, pouring the sherry. "May I ask what they're for? Knockouts?" He laughed to show he was joking.

"Knockouts is right," Bonny answered. "I got them from the doctor to make me sleep. Haven't taken them lately.

I used to take one in a glass of sherry at night. They dissolve in sherry, I found. No taste."

"Aren't they dangerous?"

"Not unless you took three or four at once. Fatal dose. Never wake up." Bonny watched the clock, waiting for Shamrock to come down. "Excuse me. I'll go see what's keeping Shamrock."

"Yes, perhaps she needs help with her dress."

After Bonny left the drawing room, the Senior carried the decanter back to the wine cabinet and there paused, staring fixedly at the small bottle of pills. Three or four, she had said, made a fatal dose. They dissolved in sherry. No taste.

That doddering old Dr. Pennyfeather might be wrong in his verdict. Bonny Belle didn't act like a dying woman. Perhaps she wouldn't die for years. If she continued to live . . .

The thought was intolerable. Fifty thousand dollars, as well as this house and everything in it, and probably other assets, bank accounts and securities that she lived on. Everything willed to the girl who today would become Mansell's wife, his quiet and obedient wife who wouldn't dare to raise a question concerning the disposal of her legacy. She'd better not.

Three or four, a fatal dose. There were five pills left in the bottle. The Senior looked at his hand, picking the bottle up, and felt pride in the fact that it was perfectly steady. Things were simplified if you coolly took advantage of opportunity. No risk to speak of. Nobody would wonder. Heart trouble. The high excitement of the wedding.

He dropped the five pills into Bonny's wineglass. He watched them dissolve, and stirred the sherry thoroughly with his forefinger. He had his own glass in his hand when Bonny came back into the drawing room.

"She'll be right down," said Bonny. "A bit shy, is all."

She picked up her wineglass and raised it. "Here's long life to the bride and groom!"

"Long life," echoed the Senior, and took pride again in the fact that he was able to sip his sherry without a tremble. It was the first killing he had ever committed personally, not by hired hands.

Watching Bonny drain her glass, he thought: *Murder is really easy. So simple.*

"Honey, you look lovely!" Bonny said as Shamrock came down the stairs. "Gorgeous! Let's hurry, everybody's waiting for us. For you, I mean."

The wedding drew toward its close. "—pronounce you man and wife," concluded the solemn voice of the minister, and Shamrock felt that he might have sounded more optimistic about it. Maybe he was sorry for the Junior. Some of the women were weeping. Probably from chagrin for their eligible daughters. A gladsome day, this. Bones! Shamrock, clearsighted, knew she was standing on reluctant sufferance because of marrying into the Keller family.

A sudden stir of commotion broke out in the church, and Shamrock turned to see what was wrong. She saw a group fluttering about somebody. Then she saw that the person was Bonny, and she hastened to her.

Bonny sat slumped, head bowed, she who always sat so jauntily erect with her golden head held high. Dr. Pennyfeather, present as a guest, bent over her, mumbling, shaking his head.

As Shamrock pushed through the surrounding group, the old medico quavered, "She's gone. All this fripperish to-do was too much. Her heart was in very bad condition. I warned her to go easy. I warned her!" He sniffed. "She's been drinking, too. Stimulating spirits. What can you expect? Gone, yes, she's gone. No heartbeat."

Hovering near, the Senior clucked his tongue. "What a pity! What a very great pity! My friends, in the midst of life we are in death."

"Amen," intoned the minister.

Shamrock cuddled limp Bonny in her arms.

Outside in the street, a stranger in town watered his wornout mount at the Bearcat trough and ran estimating eyes over the array of smart rigs and saddled horses. A rich array. He took note of activities at the church, which stood on the corner of the Keller Block, across the street from the Bearcat. A bronze plaque, set permanently and prominently in the churchyard, offered the information that the site for the church had been donated by Mansell J. Keller, Esq.

"Takes a wedding or funeral to bring out the best horseflesh," the stranger murmured to himself. "I'm in luck." The bank, on the far corner from the church, didn't interest him. All he sought here was to trade his wornout horse for a fresh one and be on his way.

He was travel-stained, sweaty. His gaunted face and bloodshot eyes bore the stamp of a young man lately deprived of sleep and food. Rangily built, wire-edged, he moved with deceptive indolence while paying hard care to his surroundings. He angled toward the church corner, picking out a plain dun gelding that had good lines and a well-shaped head. Distinctive markings on a horse were the undoing of many a man who traded without its owner's consent.

His hand was reaching to untie the dun's reins when the church began emptying. Breathing a wry sigh, he walked on along the Keller Block and took shade in the nearest store doorway, tipping back his hat, which exposed a shock of red hair in need of cutting. He saw four men carrying a woman who appeared to have fainted, people pouring after them from the church, all in a flurry of excitement.

The sight brought a grin to his lips. It beat him why women got themselves wrought up and emotionally overcome at weddings. A wedding was supposedly a joyous event full of promise for the happy couple. The four men carrying the woman looked as soberly joyless as pall bearers, and the people leaving the church were solemn in their excitement.

He would have to wait for the street to clear again, before trying for the dun or some other fresh horse. He wasn't going to risk a shooting run-out, all those women in the way. A long wait. None of the crowd showed any inclination to disperse, except a group that followed the four men to the big white house down at the south end of the street. The bride dashed from the church and hurried to overtake them, lifting up her long white gown, veil streaming. The red-haired man caught only a glimpse of her face. It seemed vaguely familiar.

## VIII

The four men bore Bonny upstairs, where Shamrock had them place her on the gilt-and-ivory bed in the master bedroom. Bonny, after paying a large price for that splendid bed, had never slept in it. It was just too grand, she had said, with its carved posts and canopy and satin spread.

Well, she would rest in it now, and it wasn't a bit too grand for her. When the four men withdrew, Shamrock stood gazing down at the white face. She smoothed back the golden hair.

"Goodby, Bonny," she whispered. "I hope it didn't hurt."

Cornelius Winterfield, of the Winterfield Funeral Parlor, came up softly into the bedroom, hat in hand. He coughed, bobbed his head to Shamrock, and cast a professional glance at the still figure on the bed.

"You'll want to make the proper arrangements for the interment of the deceased. I have several fine caskets, very high-class. Silk linings. Solid silver fittings—"

"Yes, of course. The burial." Shamrock hadn't given it a thought. There had been no time. "Please attend to it."

"Thank you, Miss O'Terran. I'll have the body removed to my premises this afternoon. Unless, that is, you prefer the services to be held here."

"No. Not here." She shrank from the thought of people, so-called mourners, parading in and out of the house. Curiosity seekers, prying, poking into Bonny's things. She was Bonny's only real mourner.

"Very well. Permit me to offer my deepest sympathy."

The undertaker backed out, bowing, leaving Shamrock standing by the bed.

Presently, sounds and murmuring voices brought Shamrock out to the head of the staircase. She looked down over the balustrade.

Downstairs, the house was alive with people who had never set foot in it before. They were examining the lavish contents, pointing and making comments, as if the house was a public museum. One woman, opening the wine cabinet, clucked her tongue at the assortment of bottles. Two others fingered Bonny's sapphire-blue velvet cloak, smiling and shaking their heads over its flamboyant richness. Bonny had loved color. The cloak had become rather worn, but she couldn't bear to part with it.

The Senior had uncovered the small steel strongbox in which Bonny stored her jewelry and other valuables. It was set into the wall and hidden behind a hanging strip of tapestry. He inspected its lock. He spoke to Mansell. Brazenly, the two of them rummaged through Bonny's dainty escritoire, obviously in search of the key.

Shamrock's eyes blazed, watching them. The prying, smirking rabble! Smug hypocrites. Pawing and criticizing Bonny's treasures, under pretension as mourners.

Shamrock fled to her own room. She tore off her bridal dress in wild anger, balling it up and kicking it across the floor. From a corner of her clothes closet she unearthed her old canvas pants and flannel shirt. The pants, last time she wore them, had to be rolled up. They fitted her now. She had grown taller, longer in the legs.

She buckled on the Captain's gunbelt and patted the well-worn holster. The weight and feel of it gave solid substance to her wrath. A remnant sense of caution raised warning, but wrath quickly killed it. She left her room and traversed the second-floor hallway to the staircase, recklessly ready to take on anyone and everyone, damn the consequences.

More people had entered. The front door hung wide open to all comers. There was nobody to stop them from handling the gorgeous furnishings, nor from taking bits of bric-a-brac as souvenirs of *That Woman*. Trifles to be giggled over later in social gatherings. Mementoes of notorious Bonny Belle Blue, who had tried to break the barriers of Piety's upper class, and failed by the provident stroke of death.

Shamrock clenched her teeth, furious at them. She loved Bonny as an older sister, almost a mother.

Mansell was first to see her descending the wide stairs. He straightened up from searching the drawers of the escritoire, his mouth open, eyes rounded at her disreputable garb.

"What the hell! Have you lost your mind?"

"No," said Shamrock. "My mind's okay. Get out of here, Junior!"

Mansell gasped. He advanced on her to the foot of the stairs. "You must be mad!"

"I'm mad, all right. Mad clear through! Get out!" she repeated. "You and your father. Everybody. Out! I'm mistress of this house."

"Pull yourself together. You're my wife! You'll do as I tell you!"

"Forget it! I wouldn't have your hide for a saddle blanket!" She surveyed him up and down with scorching contempt. Her right hand slapped her gun free of its holster, thumbing the single-action hammer to full cock on hair-trigger. "Out, you and the rest of the coyotes! Jackals! I'll give you ten seconds before I start shooting. One—two—three . . ."

The shocked women rushed out, jostling one another, babbling in near panic. Men pressed after them, attempting to retain shreds of dignity while hastening the exodus, convinced that Shamrock meant what she said. The wild girl stood within her rights. Nobody could justify flouting her command, backed by a gun, to vacate her home.

Near the church, the red-haired stranger postponed once more his taking of the dun gelding. He swore under his breath. Those people. Those clucking women. He wished they'd stay off the street and let him scoot out on the dun, no hurt to anybody. Some kind of uproar at the big white house was spilling them out.

The house cleared empty before Shamrock reached the count of ten. Closing the wine cabinet, she noticed that Bonny's pill bottle also was empty, though it had contained five pills that morning. But her rage allowed the fact scarce room for cogitation. She hurried on to slam shut the front door and bar Piety from the house.

The Senior jammed a foot against the door. His thin lips stretched white. "Girl, you need taming!" he grated, reaching to pull her out. "If my son can't do it, I can! Come with me!"

Her gun promptly blared, and he jumped back off the front steps, his wrist furrowed and running blood. The crowd outside gaped aghast.

"You damned wildcat!"

Shamrock laughed at him. "That's what I am, all right! A wildcat O'Terran!" Thumbing back the hammer of her gun, she swept her searing scorn over the crowd. "I know about your whispering and nudging. You've all been waiting, watching me, hoping I'd make a slip. Well, here it is!"

In her furious indignation she made the unthinking mistake of advancing from the house into the street. Several men moved to close in around her. She fired over their heads to discourage them, and succeeded. Her bullet crashed a window of the Keller Bank, startling a string of rack-tied horses into snapping their bridles and bolting off, spooking others that had been dozing in the hot sun.

The surrounding men flinched and fell back, Mansell among them. For good measure, having gone so far on her rampage, Shamrock triggered a second shot that whanged off the Bearcat false-front and droned sinisterly overhead. Men and women fled, dodging the runaway horses. That girl had gone crazy. She was liable to kill somebody. They shouted for the sheriff.

Into sight puffed Sheriff Blount, grown fat in his middle age, a reasonably honest law officer as long as duty didn't conflict with Keller interests. In recent years he had become more and more corrupted, shutting his eyes to the process of subtle bribes and veiled threats. His eyes now automatically sought the Senior, looking for instructions.

"Put that girl under arrest!" the Senior ordered him. "She's gone insane—a public menace! Zeigler! Where the devil are you, Zeigler?"

Jupe Zeigler, regularly employed on the Keller Bank's payroll as armed guard, came running. A taciturn and secretive man, he lived without friends, yet wielded an iron authority over the gunslung newcomers who congregated nightly in the Bearcat. No matter how drunkenly boisterous, free-spending, giving the barmen rough treatment, at Zeigler's creepy entrance they quieted down. The sheriff had come to depend on him, had appointed him deputy; to his private shame. Sheriff Blount knew that Ziegler was Keller's paid gun-boss.

Zeigler and the sheriff made straight for Shamrock on the run. Mansell sternly joined them after noting that Shamrock was having to reload her gun; she had pitched three more shots costing three more windows and causing several buckboard teams to strike driverless for home.

Somebody else loosed a shot. Shamrock looked up from

sliding fresh shells into the cylinder of her smoking gun. She enjoyed the exhilaration of shooting up this town that she hated. Her color was high. Her eyes sparkled. If anyone wished to make a serious shooting match of the frolic, she was prepared to accommodate him. The sheriff, Zeigler, Mansell, anyone.

They charged at her until the bullet from elsewhere whipped the sheriff's hat off his head. It brought them up short to a stunned standstill, glaring around in search of the shooter who dared to fire on them. A second shot spurted up dust warningly between the feet of Zeigler, who had chopped a hand hipward, and a third slashed the holster, an inch from his fingers. Zeigler snatched his hand away, knowing he was dead-marked if he tried to make good his draw.

The shooter was the red-haired stranger. Shamrock didn't recognize him, couldn't place him, and wondered fleetingly why he pitched into a fracas that didn't concern him.

He wasn't a Piety man. Definitely not. Among the common run of Piety townsmen he stood out as singular as a war-lance in a stand of umbrellas. A man accustomed to violence. A gay and lighthearted warrior, laughing while he called to her, "Don't you remember me?"

"No," she answered him.

He sagged his shoulders in exaggerated grief. "The pity of it! And me remembering you so well. Dry Spring. Union Junction. Some years back. I'm Red Mackenzie."

"The kiltie!"

"That's me, it's what you called me then. What trouble you got into here in this place, I can't guess, but kindly count me in on it." Despite the travel-worn roughness of his appearance, he still retained a courtly manner. "I'll side with you any time, any place. Where's your big friend?"

"The Lord knows!"

"Or the Devil! I've heard tell of Rogue Bishop's doings!"

They spoke together while the crowd in the street, cowed frozen by their readily cocked guns, listened wide-eyed. Zeigler shifted his feet, then he also froze carefully still, spying Red Mackenzie's gun aimed directly at him. Sheriff Blount picked up his bullet-torn hat and made a dignified ceremony of fitting it back on his head, attempting to save face. The Kellers, father and son, stood straightly like soldiers at attention.

Two men rushed out from the Bearcat. They belonged in the gun-slung breed that had lately infested Piety, but were off-duty, drinking to fill their unemployed time. They came loaded for trouble, guns out.

They promptly met it. Shamrock and Red Mackenzie both fired, fast, aiming charitably low. One of the gunmen collapsed forward, clutching his leg, mouth wide in a howl. The other threw up his hands and limped back into the Bearcat, where three more of the gun-slung breed, awakened from drunken oblivion by the shots, lurched to the batwing doors and bore him protestingly out again before them. The crowd burst apart, scampering for cover.

"Don't you dare talk against Rogue!" Shamrock severely rebuked Red Mackenzie, as if nothing of much consequence had interrupted their conversation. "He left me here soon after that Union Junction blow-up. He couldn't keep me, being what he is."

"The blackguard! The—"

"Watch it, kiltie!"

"Don't get scratchy, spud!" he retorted, discarding his courtliness, his tone of voice matching his rough looks.

"I mean watch Zeigler—that one there!"

"Beg your pardon."

Zeigler, seizing advantage of the general commotion, was attempting another play. Retreating a few steps with the mixed crowd of alarmed men and panicky women, he whirled in mid-stride with his gun out, anxious to show the Senior that he earned his wages.

To create a diversion, Shamrock blasted another window. A fleeing woman screamed. Sheriff Blount, finding himself blocking Zeigler's line of fire, jumped out of the way, bawling, "Careful, man—go careful on that! The women!"

Rogue Bishop, entering Piety in response to a formal invitation that had brought him many miles from more customary and less sedate affairs, reined his horse up short, blinking in surprise at the riotous scene before him. He had hurried to get here in time to see Shamrock in bridal dress, a blushing bride, a proper young lady to whom he would pay his grave respects and good wishes. He had looked forward to it, seeing it as the final end of his obligation, such as it was. From then on, he could put her completely out of his mind. She would be solely the responsibility of the proud and happy groom.

Instead, there she stood in the turmoil of the street, wearing her disreputable canvas pants and flannel shirt, smoking gun in hand. Piety might just as well have been Dry Spring or Union Junction. Or Candelaria, for that matter.

"What the blazes!" Bishop muttered, his wishful illusions crumbling. "This is a wedding?"

# IX

Red Mackenzie and Zeigler stared at each other over levelled guns, in a wordless duel of nerves that forbade giving the slightest heed to anything else.

A burly bartender stepped forth from the Bearcat. He brandished a sawed-off shotgun as a murderous threat, advancing toward the redhead. Inside the saloon a shadowy figure thrust the searching barrel of a rifle out through the broken window, backing the bartender's advance.

Shamrock took quick aim and squeezed the trigger. The hammer clicked on an empty chamber. She tried again, with the same result. Mansell then lunged at her, arms spread to catch and overpower his unruly bride.

She threw her left hand up as if to rake at his face. He dodged that, but not the instant move of her right hand, an accurate slam that she had put him into position to take. Her gunbarrel crushed his fine beaver hat. Mansell reeled off, holding his head, legs sagging.

The Senior called out furiously, "Get her, somebody! All of you! Get her! She's a maniac!"

Bishop swore, wanting to turn right around and pull out, foreseeing a load of profitless trouble for himself if he didn't. While trouble-shooting was his second trade, he ruled that it should produce a profit. Shamrock wasn't only a dead loss, she was a liability.

Still, he had left her in this town, palmed her off on Bonny Belle Blue. Bonny obviously hadn't made much headway in making a lady of her. Where, he wondered, was Bonny now? The girl urgently needed help, trying with her empty gun to stand off several townsmen grimly converging on her.

73

Against his better judgment, Bishop heeled his horse on forward. He swooped down on Shamrock from behind. The oncoming hoofbeats brought her to twist around from confronting the group of townsmen, who paused, eyeing askance the big rider and uncertain of his purpose. He was an unwanted intruder. The bartender tilted his fearsome weapon. The rifle muzzle in the broken window shifted.

At sight of the darkly severe garb, the rakish hat, the forbiddingly hard face, Shamrock let out the squawl of a roistering cowpuncher. "Rogue!"

Her glad welcome failed to gentle his harsh mood. He leaned over from the saddle and grabbed hold of her shirt. It tore. He got another handful of shirt and slung her up behind him, like taking a cat by the scruff of its neck, or picking up a blanket on the run.

"Get set!"

"Rogue, you hound! You ornery big hound!" She pounded his broad back. "You did come, bless you!" His chilly gray eyes and flattened lips couldn't faze her. She knew him, or thought she did.

"Save the celebration!"

He was alertly aware of the bartender and the Bearcat rifleman, both aiming at him. He drew, fired twice, snapped the long-barrelled gun cocked for further hostilities. The bartender retreated on unsteady legs. The rifle fell into the sill of the broken window.

"Hang on! We're getting out! You young hellion, I ought've known you'd never make a lady!"

Shamrock pounded his back again. "Wait, Rogue, wait! Got to give my friend a hand. He sided me."

"Friend? Who?"

"The kiltie, Red Mackenzie. That's him there."

"Holy Moses, him again?" Bishop growled, remembering a redheaded young Scot whose efforts in a couple of towns had worsened matters. "Double trouble!"

However, he reined up at Shamrock's insistence and swung back, she declaring that Red Mackenzie's life wasn't worth two cents if they left him behind. Red Mackenzie had come out of nowhere and taken up for her against the town, the sheriff, and a deputy who, she asserted, was a gun-boss.

The redhead's life wasn't worth two cents to Bishop under any circumstances that he could think of at the moment, but he called, "Get your horse, Red!" Then he took in Red's predicament, a stand-off, muzzle to muzzle, and he rapped at Zeigler, "Drop that gun and trot off!"

Zeigler did neither. He holstered his gun with care, while looking at Bishop recognizingly, then spread his hands open in a gesture of temporary defeat.

"We'll meet again, Mr. Bishop," he murmured. "It won't be long."

He turned and walked without haste toward the bank. The group of townsmen opened to let him through. To them, and to the sheriff, he said, "He got the edge on me. I don't take chances with his kind." Then to the Senior, "I'll want the men, Mr. Keller."

"Have them called in!"

"Get your horse," Bishop repeated to Red Mackenzie. "I'll cover for you." He waited only until Red got mounted on the dun, before he wheeled and took off out of town, scowling over the fact that he had once more saddled himself with this wildling waif, Shamrock, daughter of that harum-scarum soldier of fortune, Captain O'Terran.

"This feels familiar, riding behind you," Shamrock said presently. "Same horse, isn't it?"

He nodded. "Older, like me, but still got the steam. We'll need it!"

"Guess we will." She looked back through their raised dust. "Red got clear. He coming."

"That's just fine!" Bishop grunted.

More and more, he bleakly regretted responding to that formal invitation. A courtesy call was all he'd had in mind. Ride in, give her his good wishes and the wedding present he had bought for her, and ride out quickly before the assembled guests took a close look at him. He certainly hadn't intended to kidnap the bride.

"What were you shooting up the town for?" he demanded. "Isn't this your wedding day?"

"Right," Shamrock agreed. "Married at noon with all the fixings. Flowers, everything. The full works. All the best people in town there. Too bad you missed it. You should have seen me."

Red Mackenzie caught up on the dun and fell into gait alongside, listening. Shamrock scanned his face and eyes, and exchanged a grin with him.

"The wedding wasn't exactly my idea. I did it to please Bonny." She paused. "After I shot the Senior—my father-in-law, that is—"

"You what?" Bishop turned his head to look at her. "Kill him?"

" 'Fraid not."

He let that pass. "Who was the dressed-up duck you conked on the head?"

"That was my husband."

"Hell of a honeymoon!"

She laughed. "I sort of annulled the marriage, you might say."

"Where's Bonny?" Bishop asked. "I didn't see her."

Shamrock's eyes clouded. "Bonny died today, Rogue. Died in church during the wedding. Too much excitement, the doctor said. She had a weak heart."

Bishop took off his hat, wiped the sweatband, and put it back on. "Never knew there was anything wrong with

Bonny's heart. In Tombstone she . . ." He didn't finish that, muttering, "Sorry she's gone."

They fell silent, riding steadily southward. Shamrock slipped her hands up onto Bishop's shoulders, shifting her comfortless seat, and he leaned back a little.

Red Mackenzie dropped to the rear. When he caught up again later, he remarked, "I think there's a posse after us, or something of the kind. Quite a dust cloud it makes. Gaining on us. Our dust and our tracks in this sand are too easy to follow, Mr. Bishop, don't you think so?"

Bishop surveyed the broken skyline ahead. "I think so," he answered, unwittingly picking up the redhead's manner of speech. "We'll cut west to Stone Flats, then circle back round to the ridges, south there. With any luck, it'll throw them off. They'll wear out their horses before dark. Suit you?"

"Anything you say, Mr. Bishop."

A certain clippedness in the young man's voice caused Bishop to glance querying at him. "Something bothering you?"

Red Mackenzie took his eyes off Shamrock, whose hands stayed clasped on Bishop's shoulders. "It's personal, Mr. Bishop," he replied, and dropped back once more.

Bishop shrugged warily. His well-meant visit to Piety had taken on the unlucky aspects of a Captain O'Terran venture, one misfortune after another. It was plain that Red Mackenzie held romantic notions about Shamrock. Strong notions. And probably he was afflicted by a Scottish sense of morality: the moral sense that condoned horse-stealing and other such felonies, but sternly condemned virile looseness—the more sternly when he was cut out.

Feeling Bishop's shrug beneath her clasping hands,

Shamrock looked back at Red Mackenzie in the rear and said, "He's mad at you, Rogue. Mad at me, too."

"You know why," Bishop growled. "Keep your hands to yourself!"

He couldn't see the impish delight that sparkled her eyes. She was entirely feminine underneath the hoydenish surface.

"He's jealous!"

"Yeah, and he's got a gun. He's behind me." A jealous man, armed, was the most dangerous of all men. Morals and ethics then failed.

"I'll watch him."

"You do that!"

They made a hidden camp between rocky ridges. A small fire in a scoop of ground, Indian-like. They fanned the wisps of smoke, not allowing the smoke to raise a tell-tale column in the still air. The sun sank low and the evening breeze blew up to let them relax in the shadow of the ridges. Only by sheer luck could the Piety hunters discover them here.

Shamrock told the rest of her story. She sat on her heels, sipping hot coffee made from stone-crushed beans, black as night and unsweetened. Thoroughly at ease, she gazed fondly at the two men, a hard-looking pair. Any other girl would have fled screaming.

Bishop, with his build, his strength, his darkly sardonic face, had somewhat the appearance of a devil who, ruthless, untroubled by scruples, had come to earth to wreak violence. The deepening shadow filled the creases and lines of his face. No longer could he count himself young. Yet in the count of years he wasn't old. Hardbitten experience had aged him.

Red Mackenzie looked as if he never should have come in out of the chaparral.

A pair of wild hawks. Her own kind of people. Shamrock understood them, understood perfectly their way of life. She was infinitely more comfortable with them, here in an outlaw camp, than she had ever felt in Piety. There was no food except a few scraps of jerky produced by Bishop along with the roasted coffee beans—his emergency rations—and for bedding they would have to use the ground. But she had regained what she rated was freedom, the free life such as she had enjoyed all through her earlier years with Captain O'Terran.

She as born to it, Bishop mused. An incorrigible wildling. It was in her blood. He lighted up a thin cigar and asked Red Mackenzie, "You on the dodge?"

"If I wasn't before around noon today," Red answered, "I most certainly am now!"

"That makes three of us," Shamrock observed. "Robbed any good banks lately?"

Red shook his head. "You misjudge me. Admitted, some laws lie broken behind me. Too many. Outright robbery, no." He rolled a brown cigarette, saying seriously, "I get into scrapes, often from letting myself become involved in somebody else's misfortunes."

"So I noticed today. And five years ago."

"It's a habit I must break."

"You remind me of my father. He never broke the habit of helping the underdog."

"Ah, there are underdogs everywhere you turn. The struggling homesteaders. The widows with children to feed. Indians trying to fit in, against prejudice and persecution. You can't help them all. They've cost me a few fine jobs, here and there. I'm a good cowman, flat broke, wanted for horse-stealing and other felonies! That's all the habit got me!" Red stopped.

Changing the subject, he asked Shamrock, "What do you aim to do with yourself?"

She blinked at the abrupt question. "I figured to trail along with you two."

Bishop and Red clashed glances. They brought their eyes to bear meditatively on her. Their problem child. More than a child. Much more. Bishop, conscious of her womanliness, puffed smoke to hide his faint smile at the idea of the three of them journeying amicably together night and day.

"A young girl can't go camping around with two men!" Red stated flatly. "It's—it's—"

"Awkward," Bishop supplied.

" 'Scandalous' is the word I wanted."

"Try 'dangerous.' It's more fitting."

Shamrock bent her head. "All right. I'll pick up a horse somewhere and make for California."

"Nor can a young girl go traipsing cross-country all by herself!"

"This one would, if I let her."

"If *you* let her? Mr. Bishop, you don't own her!"

"Get this straight, buster," said Bishop. "I took her in tow when her hell-raising father got killed in a running fight with Rurales. She takes after him. A sprig from a poison oak! But she's in my care, for better or worse, regardless."

"You're not her legal guardian," Red argued.

"Damn the legalities! She'll do as I tell her, within reason, or I'll turn her over my knee! She knows it."

"You won't do it while I'm alive!"

"I'll keep that in mind."

Already, the friction. Two males, one female. Shamrock smiled without resentment at Bishop. Trying to spread peace, she paid Red Mackenzie the same smile.

"If you won't let me go to California, then what? I'll just have to hang-and-rattle along with you, that's all. Suits me. Let's think of me as a man. I'm fit and able to do my share of anything, anywhere. You know that, Rogue."

It wouldn't work. Bishop bit on his cigar and spat

flakes of tobacco. Impossible to think of her as a man. Too feminine. Too damned attractive. Two virile males and a young female, journeying together, camping together. Gunpowder was less explosive, lighted match to fuse. A short fuse.

She didn't have any cash. And Red was broke, from the looks of him. Bishop, himself, wore a money belt that was lean and light, he having run into a streak of bad luck lately, the cards poor, and nobody requiring his highly paid services as a trouble-shooter. A rare state of affairs.

"Do you want to go off, leaving Bonny's money behind?" he asked Shamrock. "You tell me she willed it to you."

"And the house, everything."

"You can't take the house with you. But you could use the fifty thousand dollars she handed over to—what's his name?"

"Mansell J. Keller, Senior. He endorsed Bonny's check and cashed it. I saw it when the bank returned it, canceled. Bonny locked it in the wall safe with her jewels."

"It's proof he got her money," Red commented.

"Much good that does!" Shamrock said. "I creased the Senior, clouted Junior, and shot up the town. I don't see myself going back there and asking the Senior to kindly fork over."

Bishop gazed upward. "That, from one who bears the name of O'Terran!" he murmured to the darkening sky. "The proud stock runs to seed!"

Shamrock's head rose. "What do you mean by that?"

"I mean you're not the fighter your father was. It's only natural, though, I guess. You're just a girl, and I left you too long in Piety. The Captain was all man, no quitter. He wouldn't have quit his rights to fifty thousand dollars and a cache of jewels. Bonny's taste in jewelry ran to diamonds, I recall. Probably worth another fifty thousand."

"Are you daring me?" Shamrock flared. "Daring me to go back and try to collect?"

"Now wait a minute—!" Red began.

Bishop flapped a hand at him. "You shut up! None of your business, this." To Shamrock he said blandly, "I'm not trying to sway you. Far be it from me. It's your inheritance, the money, the jewels. Let Keller have it, if that's your wish."

"It's not my wish, but—"

"Okay, then you want to collect what's rightly yours. I'll lend a hand. All the way, kid."

Shamrock's eyes sparkled. "Rogue, you hound, you fenced me into it deliberately! I'm game to try, with you by me!"

*Bueno!*" Bishop breathed. "Red, you can check out if the game looks too tough for your constitution."

Red Mackenzie, squatting at the small fire, hunched back on his heels. "Funny thing," he said meditatively, "I was making for California when I hit Piety. After, let me admit, searching everywhere for a certain girl. I gave up hope at last of ever finding her. I came upon her in Piety, of all places."

He raised his eyes from the fire. "Count me in. All the way, Mr. Bishop, like yourself."

"If we collect, we split it even," Shamrock proposed. She sent Red a soft glance in payment for his words. "Agreed?"

Bishop made no promises, giving only a noncommittal grunt, privately ruling out Red Mackenzie. Bonny's money and jewels would make it possible to settle Shamrock somewhere far from Piety. To persuade her to stay put and behave posed a problem in itself. And Keller's son would always have a claim on her, his lawfully wedded wife, if he tracked her down.

Those were difficulties for the unknown future. The first logical move was to try collecting Shamrock's legacy for her. Bishop held to a lasting confidence in cash as the solution to most problems.

"You mentioned a wall safe where Bonny kept her jewels and put the canceled check that Keller cashed," he said to Shamrock. "Does the safe have a regular lock, or a combination?"

"A lock. Bonny carried the key on a thin gold chain around her neck, underneath her dress. Always. She wasn't ever careless with it."

"Knowing Bonny, I bet she wasn't."

"The key ought to be still there under her dress, unless Winterfield, the undertaker, took it off. I doubt that. He was to move Bonny's body to his morgue this afternoon. He won't prepare her for burial till tomorrow."

Bishop emptied the coffee grounds onto the fire. "We'll find out if Bonny's still wearing the key."

"Tonight?" Red exclaimed. "Back to Piety, and a Piety posse hunting us? It's shoving our heads into the lion's mouth!" Then he nodded. "Ah, well—why not? Tonight it is!"

"I can't think of a better time, the funeral tomorrow or the day after," said Bishop. "Let's saddle up."

# X

Breaking at night into a funeral parlor wasn't one of Bishop's varied proclivities. He did possess a trained talent for getting anywhere he determined to go, and the bolt on the side window proved amenable to his knife. He raised the window and eased his large frame over the sill.

Shamrock followed him in, then Red Mackenzie, who shut down the window, making a slight noise. They stood listening while they adjusted their eyes to the gloom. The front windows, half-curtained with a flimsy purple material, allowed a dim illumination to penetrate from the iron lantern that always hung lighted all night before the bank on the other side of the street. The room was cluttered. Winterfield used it partly as a workshop.

Empty coffins rested on trestles painted black, the lids open in somber invitation. Others, unfinished, were piled against a wall. Winterfield believed in preparedness for any rush in trade. Metal handles and plates of varying cost were laid out ready for the choice of mourners who could afford to pay for them. The floor was littered with wood shavings.

Bishop drew down the corners of his wide mouth in rank distaste. The place reeked of the cold formalities of death, the impersonal workmanship that laid a corpse for pay into its grave. A damnably dismal finish to a red-blooded life. For himself, when he reached his end, he would prefer to meet it somewhere out in the careless solitude of the desert, or in some barranca of the badlands, hidden away in privacy. Bonny would have liked that, too, but she had made the unfortunate error of dying in Piety.

Two other sets of black trestles, bearing wooden slabs, were screened off from the front of the room by a drably painted partition. The morgue. The slabs held two human shapes covered with white sheets. Two corpses to be readied for burial tomorrow. In this hot climate a corpse had to be buried hurriedly.

Bishop pointed at a thin crack of light in the rear of the funeral parlor. "Quiet!"

The crack of light marked the location of Winterfield's office. From behind the closed door came muffled voices, rising and falling in argument. Two voices.

Shamrock tiptoed to the partitioned-off morgue.

Bishop watched her. The girl didn't have a squeamish nerve in her body, through he knew she was capable of deeply intense feeling. She had inherited the philosophy of her father. With all his faults, Captain O'Terran had taken a commonsense attitude toward death.

Chairs scraped. The door of Winterfield's office swung open, letting in a broad fan of light. "No, I can't agree with your diagnosis," Winterfield said over his shoulder as he entered. "Blacksnake Billy simply died from too much booze. He was a drunken moocher, calling himself a Christianized Indian. These Apache heathens don't change, Alfred."

"You're an undertaker, not a doctor!" snapped old Dr. Pennyfeather, following behind him. "Alcohol caused the hardening of his liver, but it was a gradual process over the years. I know cirrhosis when I see it."

"Your eyesight isn't what it used to be."

"I'm not blind! His spleen—" The doctor fetched up with a bump against the undertaker's back, jolting both of the argumentative old cronies. "Confound it, Cornelius, what did you stop so quick for? Made me drop my glasses."

Cornelius Winterfield didn't respond. His skinny head was craned forward. He peered at a tall apparition that had no earthly right to occupy his funeral parlor. The apparition, black and motionless, met his look with a gray stare. He shrank back, losing interest in further bickering over the cause of Blacksnake Billy's demise.

"Stand still, will you?" the doctor fretted behind him, searching the floor. "You'll step on my glasses!"

Winterfield recovered a stammering trace of his voice. "W-what—who's that?" He glimpsed Red Mackenzie, then Shamrock. "Good God, w-what is this?"

"Spooks, visiting a friend," said Bishop, a touch of macabre humor leavening his mood. He asked Shamrock, "Is that Bonny there?"

"No," she answered, replacing the sheet on the first body that she investigated. "It's a drunk-dead Indian in a frowzy red blanket. Pickled in alcohol, from the smell. Phew!"

"Eh? What's that?" Dr. Pennyfeather found his glasses, undamaged. He fitted them on. He blinked through them mistily at Shamrock in her pants and shirt. "Young man, that Indian died of cirrhosis of the liver! The symptoms are plain to a trained eye such as mine. My diagnosis—"

"Whatever the sorry redskin died of," Shamrock broke into the doctor's testy tirade, "it doesn't matter. He's dead, stinking dead. Poor company for Bonny. The church will pay for his burial, I suppose."

She went to the second slab in the partitioned morgue and drew the white sheet from the head of the body that was shrouded there, uncovering a golden head.

"This," she said softly, "is Bonny."

Her voice broke. She cuddled the body to her, as if her own warmth might restore life to it. "Oh, Bonny, Bonny! I can't leave you here! I can't!"

Winterfield sidled uncertainly forward, recognizing Shamrock chiefly by her voice. He eyed askance Bishop and Red Mackenzie, her raffish companions, hardly knowing what to make of them. Still, the girl was a customer.

On that score he could overlook peculiarities of behavior, including unlawful entry into his premises, if she was able to pay for services rendered.

"Er—I haven't yet begun to prepare the body. I was waiting for someone to guarantee the payment of—I mean, someone to, er, to stand responsible. You see, Miss, er, Mrs. Keller, excuse me, there are—"

Bishop waved him quiet. "We understand. No pay, no coffin, nothing. Roll her body into an arroyo, if the town stands for it. I guess this lousy town just might!"

Gazing with unreadable eyes at the white blur of Bonny's face, he murmured, "Goddam fine Christians! Can you find the key on her, Shamrock?"

"No. It's gone!"

"The buzzards got here before us, kid!"

Shamrock turned on Winterfield. "She wore a little key on a thin gold chain around her neck. The key to her private strongbox in the house. She wore it even to the wedding. I saw it! We helped each other dress."

"I—I . . ." Winterfield stuttered. "A key?"

"Yes, a key," Bishop said tonelessly. He slid a hand under his ministerial coat. "Somebody took it. Ghouls who rob the dead deserve killing. You?"

"No, no, I didn't take it!" Winterfield protested. "I swear I didn't!" He cringed from Bishop's cold glare.

"Then who?"

"The Senior. Mr. Keller. He came in to view the body and say a prayer. His prayer was beautiful, sir, really quite beautiful. Biblical. When he left, I saw him put something gold in his coat pocket."

"You didn't stop him? Didn't ask him what it was he'd taken from a body in your charge?"

"Sir, we don't question the Senior! I supposed he had taken a keepsake. He and Miss Blue had lately become friends. Close friends. Everyone knew that."

Bishop looked at Shamrock, who was smoothing Bonny's hair. "We're too late! Keller got the key He's looted that strongbox by now. Bonny's jewels, the canceled check—" He stopped speaking as a loud knock hit the front door.

"Now we're in for it!" said Red Mackenzie. He cocked the hammer of his gun. "I hate like hell to shoot at ordinary citizens. How about you, Mr. Bishop?"

"I feel the same way."

The building echoed hollowly to a repeated banging on the door. Men's profiles shadowed the thin curtains of the front windows. A mob. Gunmetal reflected glints from the Keller Bank's iron lantern. An armed mob.

"On the other hand, Mr. Bishop, do they strike you as ordinary citizens? Tame townsmen?"

"Not all of 'em. Some."

"Mr. Winterfield!" boomed the voice of Sheriff Blount. "Open up! Paco Galindo, here, he vows he saw a break-in! Three burglars. Right, Paco?"

"Si, señor. One was ver' big. Two times my heavy. I tol' you. Black."

At the same time, a pungent and unladylike word came from Shamrock. She stepped back hurriedly from stroking Bonny's hair and straightening her rumpled dress. She looked scared.

"Godllemighty!"

Bonny Belle Blue rose slowly on the morgue slab, moaning.

Dr. Pennyfeather stared in stark outrage at the woman he had pronounced dead, his stubborn mind rejecting any possibility that he could have made a mistake. A corpse was required to rest decently still, once he signed the death certificate.

"I don't believe it!" he stated. "This is a trick! A lowdown trick to undermine my professional standing! That woman is dead!"

Winterfield, having a different type of mind, mumbled, "No, Alfred, she's alive. She's getting up, see? It's—it's most unusual. I've never before—"

The full shock of it choked his speech. He stood gaping as Bonny sat up on the slab. Tomorrow was her funeral, in the event that someone guaranteed the bill.

Bonny gazed unseeingly about her with dazed, wandering eyes. Her teeth chattered. She was crying. The tears drenched her white face.

"I'm c-c-cold!" she moaned.

Winterfield turned and scurried for the front door. The doctor glared indignantly at Bonny. Red Mackenzie launched a bulldogging tackle that brought Winterfield down. The banging fists shook the door. Someone rammed a shoulder at it. Faces pressed close against the windows, trying to make out what was going on inside.

"Open up, Mr. Winterfield! This is the sheriff!"

"He knows that, if he can hear!" jeered a voice. "Bust the door!"

"I don't have legal cause to. It's only Paco's word." Sheriff Blount, much as he had compromised his integrity under pressure, could revert to strict legality when it didn't clash with Keller designs. "Dr. Pennyfeather, are you in there? If you are, let us in."

Shamrock slid out her gun. "Don't you make a move to that door!" she warned the snorting doctor. "Bonny! Heaven's sake, Bonny, are you really alive?"

"C-cold," Bonny complained, shivering miserably, tugging the shrouding sheet around her. She got her bare feet to the floor and stood swaying. Her blue eyes, drug-blurred, swam with the vacant gaze of a baby. She was chilled through, her sluggishly beating heart having all it could do to combat the depressant effects of the near-fatal dose that the Senior had slipped into her glass.

Bishop peered briefly out the window by which he

had made forced entry, and drew back. There were men also in the side alley. He passed on into Winterfield's office, blew out the lamp, and inspected the rear. More men there, and more joining them. They had the place surrounded.

Chewing on an unlighted cigar, Bishop backed into the funeral parlor. The question was what to do about Bonny. If it were only himself and Red Mackenzie, with Shamrock doing her part, the three of them might manage to pull a break-out. It wasn't possible while they were encumbered with a semi-conscious woman whose first need was medical care.

Rock-bottom logic ruled that she must be left behind. She hadn't given the law of this town any reason to harass her. Yet the decision came hard. She had been robbed of her money and jewels by Keller. She would be alone, ill, helpless to whatever Keller did to silence her.

## XI

As he re-entered the funeral parlor Bishop became sharply aware that Bonny had wandered away from the morgue slab. She was at the front door, fumbling back the bolt.

"Stop, Bonny!" He leaped after her, too late.

Bonny got the door open, not hearing or not heeding him. She had found an escape from this dark, unfamiliar place. Red Mackenzie, busy quieting Winterfield without doing him serious damage, hadn't noticed; nor Shamrock, holding the doctor at bay.

Bonny Belle Blue craved the warm comfort of her bed. She tottered out, hugging the white sheet around her, oblivious of the gaping mob in the street. Bishop, stopping short of the open door, watched her pause like a lost wraith seeking its bearings. A hush descended on the mob. For a sudden moment all sound and animation died. Then she swayed forward a few steps. Men edged away from her. Sheriff Blount half-raised an arm in a gesture of astonished protest. Paco Galindo hurriedly crossed himself.

Bonny spied her big white house. Uttering a hollow sob of gladness, she drifted uncertainly in its direction. She stretched out her shrouded arms as if to embrace it, her haven from the bewildering nightmare behind her.

Shamrock brushed past Bishop, running to the door. He hauled her back. She fought against him, writhing like a captured cat to break his hold.

"Let me go, Rogue!"

"Not out there, barefaced to the sheriff's crowd!"

"I've got to help Bonny! She needs me!"

"Quiet!" he muttered. He carried her kicking to the partitioned morgue. He whisked the smelly old blanket off the body of Blacksnake Billy. "Wear it. Keep your face covered. Maybe it'll fool them till you reach the house. Two spooks are better'n one."

Shamrock arranged the blanket so that it cloaked her from head to foot and shielded her face. "This okay?"

"Okay. Try not to trip on it. Don't run. Walk. Take small steps, slow."

"How about you and Red?"

She had her father's trait of giving concern to friends in a tight pinch. It wasn't uncommon among the wild breed. When carried to extremes, Bishop reflected, it became foolhardy. "We'll make out," he said with somewhat higher optimism than he felt.

"Will I see you again?" she asked in a small and muffled voice. "Ever?"

"You know it, kid."

"Soon?"

"You bet."

"Good! *Bueno* to hell!" The old diehard phrase of speech, coined below the border. "Well, here goes!"

"No!" Red Mackenzie objected. He held a hand clamp over Winterfield's mouth, while keeping an eye on the doctor. "You can't, Shamrock! You'll—"

"Save your breath," Bishop cut him off. "She's gone."

Leaving the funeral parlor, Shamrock appeared to glide over the ground, an illusion created by sliding her feet to avoid treading on the dragging blanket. She kept her hooded head bowed, shadowing her face from the light of the Keller Bank's iron lantern.

Bishop murmured to Red Mackenzie, "She's doing all right so far. They don't know what to make of it." He held a gun in readiness for anyone opposing the girl. "Don't you let that body-snatcher spoil it."

"Tend to your own stew, Mr. Bishop, I can tend to mine! What's happening now out there? I don't hear anything. Not a sound. Like a graveyard."

"She's spooking them."

A kind of sigh whooshed from the men in the street, standing frozen. They had seen clearly the white face of Bonny Belle Blue, a walking corpse. They couldn't see the dark and unlovely visage of Blacksnake Billy, but imagination made it visible. His grubby Indian blanket was a sore sight to everyone in Piety except the pastor, who, believing he had made a convert of the tramp, had welcomed him into his flock. Blacksnake Billy was now dead, unquestionably dead. The churchgoers had thankfully raised a subscription to provide for his burial.

And here he came, another walking corpse. Ghastly deliberate, it glided toward Paco Galindo. The young Mexican, imbued with an ages-old horror of Apaches, besides a belief in the supernatural powers of the restless dead, cowered behind Sheriff Blount.

The sheriff moved aside. His stolid nature rejected superstition, but his senses revolted against any contact with the unearthly shape approaching.

Left unprotected, Paco Galindo fled, howling low. The slapping of his feet sounded like a cane whipped along the palings of a picket fence. Several men were not too proud to follow him, though lacking his speed. Doubtless, later they would swear they had gone after Paco to bring him back as a witness. They never caught him. Bonny Belle Blue, reaching her house, pushed open the front door and toppled inside, tripping on the doorstep. The door stayed open after she fell in.

Shamrock floated to the house, playing her part. The heads of all the remaining men in the street turned, eyes fixed on her. At the last bit of a moment she hurried. She picked up the dragging ends of the blanket. She ran to Bonny, to Bonny lying dazed in the entrance hall of the house. Doing that, Shamrock wasn't a spectre. She was human. And feminine.

"That ain't the Injun!" a man exclaimed, voicing the general change of opinion. "Sheriff, you've been humbugged!" So had all the rest been humbugged, but they weren't about to admit it. On the contrary.

"I knew it wasn't no ghost! Pah!"

"Who said it was? Not me!"

"No such things as ghosts."

"Nor walking corpses. Stands to reason."

"Sure. When they're dead, they're dead. They don't move, none I ever saw."

"How about the Blue woman?"

"Well . . ."

Sheriff Blount, his ordinary composure largely restored, called to Shamrock, "Stop, you! Stop right there!"

Shamrock darted on into the house and slammed the door shut. The sheriff plodded onward, frowning at the flout to his command. Uncertain of what lawful charges he could impose on a bogus ghost, he paused, saying testily to the men crowding after him, "Now, wait a minute! Don't push me!"

In the funeral parlor, Bishop muttered, "Now's the time! Let's get! Hit the thick of 'em, no try to fade out—it wouldn't work. Ready, Red?"

"Ready!"

Bishop drew his brace of long-barrelled guns as he stepped forth, fired two shots into the air, and for good measure uttered a full-throated bellow that caused even Red Mackenzie to blink.

They tore into the midst of the thunderstruck crowd like a pair of wild bulls. Slashing right and left, Bishop burst through and ducked off into the vacant gap between Schmidt's Emporium and the saddle shop. The element of surprise had its limitations. A wise veteran of violence learned to distrust it beyond its calculated span.

Red Mackenzie paused to pitch a shot backward and sprinted after him. He was laughing quietly when he caught up with Bishop on the way to the cottonwoods below town where they had hidden their horses.

"Losh, such a barney!" he panted. "A grand side-kick you'd be, Mr. Bishop. If I liked you. Which I don't, to be frank about it."

"The feeling's mutual."

"With mutual regard, at any rate. I confess she—the blonde lady—gave me a shock, rising from the dead as she did. We Scots have a superstitious streak. Half of me wanted to jump out the window. You took it in stride."

"Sure," said Bishop, unashamedly taking unearned credit. "Bonny wasn't dead. She acted doped. Somebody must have slipped her a heavy knockout, to kill her off." His deepset eyes flared. "Keller, most likely. He's got her money."

They mounted their horses. Behind them the town raised a confused din of yelling voices, running feet, stamping hoofs. A man barked orders. The Senior, no doubt. Pulling some sort of organization out of turmoil, by force of will and prestige. Rallying his undercover crew of gun hirelings, the Bearcat mob.

Looking back through the cottonwoods Bishop made out the roof of Bonny's house. Red, too, looked back, saying, "We took their minds off Shamrock. It's only temporary, though. I'm game to go back for her."

Bishop shook his head. "No good. Bonny's in poor shape. Shamrock wouldn't quit her. That's providing you got to the house alive. They're forming up a posse in the street. Sheriff's posse. Volunteer guns. Mostly Keller's, bet your boots. In a minute they'll be on our necks, all out to prove they don't know what scare is."

"Meaning we quit?"

"No, we retire for the time being. We ki-yi the hell

out of here. Come on!" Bishop gave a yank to the broad brim of his hat, settled into the saddle, and heeled the big black to a lope, its favorite gait that it could maintain for hours on end. Bishop suspected his horse of sometimes rocking itself to sleep under him.

Red Mackenzie, no novice at throwing off pursuit without crippling his mount, mentally bowed to a master of the art when they halted to air the saddle blankets and take a breather.

"Got any notion of where we are?" he queried, skeptical of the big man's talents in that respect. They had twisted and turned and retraced until his sense of direction went lost. The country all looked much the same in the darkness: barren flats, gaunt hills, dry arroyos, rocks and cactus. Hungry country, unfit for man or beast.

Bishop nodded. "Those dark blobs yonder, they're the Pedrogosas. Hold them as a landmark in case we happen to get separated. Piety's southeast of us. Not far. We circled, if you remember."

"We did. We sure did. Couple times."

"Only once. Tomorrow," Bishop continued, "we'll be hot. The Piety posse only gave up on account of the dark. Come sunup, they'll cut our sign. Not only that. The word will spread fast. Every lawman'll be on the *cuidado*, from the Swisshelms to the New Mexican line and down to the border."

"The damn' telegraph, aye. Da-da-da-dee, dot-dot. An infamous invention."

"Telegraph or not, you can't play hell with a town like Piety and expect to ride off carefree," Bishop said. "Things are changing. Where've you been these last five years?"

"Oh, around," Red answered vaguely. "Up and down, doing this and that. I skinned out of New Mexico a few days ago. Had a run-in with some local politicians there. A land-grabbing ring. It got hot."

He built a cigarette and cupped a match to it. The flare showed laughter in his eyes.

"I planned to travel straight through Arizona and on up to Nevada, maybe California. My intention was to shy clear of any trouble, as much as possible. Hah! 'The best-laid plans of mice and men . . .' Here I am again, already in bad."

"And in bad company," Bishop added for him. "But you've got a good horse." He stretched a pointing arm northward. "Up there beyond the Pedrogosas are the Chiricahuas. Rough country. Toward the north end of the Chiricahuas there's what was once an old Apache stronghold. I've used it a time or two. So have others. A man can hide there while resting his horse for the next lap. It's safe."

"I've heard of it." The tip of Red's cigarette glowed twice before he spoke next. "If Keller tried to kill Bonny, as you figure, it's reasonable to suppose he'll try again. And there's Shamrock. We left them in a tight spot."

"We left the money and jewels, too!"

"Yes, so we did." The dryness of Red's tone carried a clear implication: *Leave it to you to think of that!* "Do you aim to head for the Chiricahuas?"

Bishop's eyes glinted frostily in the darkness. "No. I was giving you directions."

"Will you take another crack at Piety? We went back and got out again. They won't be caught napping a second time. It's bloody madness to try, of course. Still, a man must do what he feels is—"

"That old Apache stronghold is safer by far."

"I doubt if I could find my way alone to it," Red stated solemnly. "Piety is a lot closer."

"A minute ago you were griping about getting in trouble. Piety is real trouble!"

"That's just what I got through saying. Bloody madness, I called it. So why will you take such a risk? Is it for the money and jewels? Surely Keller has the loot stored away tight in the bank vault."

"Your tongue will get you killed, buster!" growled Bishop, angered by the question. "I promised Shamrock I'd come back. That's enough from you!"

"And I promised myself the same thing." Their eyes met, clashed. "Lead on, Mr. Bishop. Nowhere you go is too tough for me."

"We'll see."

# XII

The only sounds of wakeful life in Piety came from the Bearcat barroom, and they were muted down to an occasional low mumble. Even that was unusual, considering the hour. On the other side of the street the Keller Bank's lantern spread its pool of light, with a dark core formed by the shadow of the lantern's big round base, like a mammoth bull's-eye.

"Wonder how many are in the barroom," Red murmured. "Be a break for us if all the posse is there, killing time, waiting for daylight. Hope so."

A faint light showed at an upstairs window of Bonny's house. Scanning the house and its surroundings, Bishop couldn't detect any movement. Nevertheless, his estimate of explosive potentialities ran high. Sensing his wary mood, Red hitched up his gunbelt. They stood by their horses under the cottonwoods.

"What do you think, Mr. Bishop?"

"I think your hope is a shade optimistic," Bishop replied judiciously. "For all we know, there could be half a dozen rifles covering Bonny's house. We might have been spotted coming here. Maybe the barroom's a plant."

He didn't believe that a man like Keller would allow his men of the posse to loaf in the Bearcat. Not this night. Keller would have some of them stationed in strategic places, on watch, as precaution if nothing else. He couldn't let down as long as a couple of hostile gunslingers, friends of Bonny and Shamrock, were on the loose.

"Mr. Bishop, you sound cautious."

"Mr. Mackenzie," said Bishop, matching Red's cool formality of speech, "caution's a good thing at times." Vigilance was part of the price he paid for his continued existence. "My hunch is that the damn town's loaded and cocked, set for us to show ourselves. I may be wrong."

"We're got to find out. Can't hang around here till morning."

"There's a sure way to find out."

They studied again what they were able to see of the house and its surroundings. "A sure way," Red agreed. "Lend me your rifle. I'll cover for you. Soon's you get there, I'll—"

"I had it in mind to do you that favor."

Both grinned faintly. Neither of them was troubled by nerves, but the darkness around the house shrieked of hidden danger. A fight was a fight. Walking into snipers' sights was suicidal.

"One of us goes first to test the lay. No percentage in us both getting killed, if there's a bushwhack." Bishop drew a deck of cards from his inside coat pocket. He slipped them out of their pack. "Cut for it? Low card goes first."

"Okay, I'm on." Red watched him shuffle and trim the deck. He took a cut and showed his card.

Bishop glanced at it. Jack of Hearts to beat. He made his cut and turned up the King of Spades.

Red nodded. He left without a word, stepping forward to the edge of the cottonwoods. Watching him go, Bishop idly riffled the deck of cards, his eyes stony. The lower end of the street, broad and bare, ran on to become the trail south. It was Red's choice whether to cross here or try it farther down. The longer course, costing time, offered only a temporary delay in testing the hazards of approaching the house.

Red chose the direct course. He stepped forward, cast a quick look left and right, and kept on going, holding himself to an easy walk that was intended to delude any watching eyes. Detachedly, Bishop gave him credit, knowing that his casual air cloaked taut alertness, stretched nerves, an anticipation of bullets tearing into his body at any instant.

Midway across the street Red's pace hastened. No burst of blazing guns met him. It gave a lift to his confidence, bolstered his hope that the men of the posse were all loafing in the Bearcat. He strode on, dropping the pretense of casualness.

Against the white house he showed as starkly plain a target as a stag in a snow-patch. The hush stayed unbroken. He reached the front door, and Bishop saw him push it open. It was unlocked, unbolted, an invitation to enter. Bishop recalled distinctly telling Shamrock to lock herself and Bonny in the house. The door became a black rectangle, opening onto darkness. It closed again and was white, blank.

Waiting, Bishop absently continued exercising his long fingers, shuffling and cutting the cards, every cut producing the King of Spades. Caution, as he had remarked to Red, was a good thing at times. Red should have taken the hint.

A noisy commotion broke the quietness, the commotion of a fight in the dark, men grunting and slugging. Overturned furniture crashed. At a gunshot it subsided to a rumble of voices. Lights presently came on in the house.

"Too bad," Bishop muttered. Regret, or something akin to it, touched him fleetingly before his face hardened, eyes bleakly opaque. Having a healthy opinion of his own worth as a lone-handed troubleshooter. he judged Red Mackenzie to be the logical sacrifice, as long as it had to be one of them.

"Better him than me."

Men were coming down the street from the Bearcat, drawn by the sounds of the brief fight and the gunshot that ended it. He gathered up the reins of the two horses and led them back out of the cottonwoods. Red was past helping. Maybe Shamrock and Bonny were, too, Keller's men occupying the big white house.

In that case, one task remained to be done. One grim task. Settle the score with Keller Senior . . .

The Senior sat in his bank office, smiling at the canceled check in his hand, the check for fifty thousand dollars that Bonny had given him to invest for her, that he had endorsed and cashed. To invest. His smile deepened. The money, in large bills, was locked in the vault with her jewelry, destined to cover shortages and satisfy the bank examiners when they arrived to inspect the books. An excellent investment, tiding him over the few months needed to complete his manipulations and reap the harvest of rangelands and town properties.

He leaned over his desk and held the canceled check above the glass chimney of the lamp. It curled in the heat, browned, flared up. He let it flutter to the floor and burn out, then tamped the crinkled black ash to a powder under his toe. Leaning back in the swivel chair, he released a sigh of deep satisfaction. There went the evidence, his signed endorsement.

The Tombstone bank had a record of the withdrawal, of course, but had no reason for producing it unless Bonny Belle Blue raised trouble. She would have to start a lawsuit, a long and involved process, costly. The Senior wondered how much more money that fantastic woman had on deposit in the Tombstone bank.

At the back of his mind was the thought that it was time for Zeigler to come and make his report. Several minutes had gone by since the commotion down at the end of the street. All was quiet again. A few inquiring townsmen had returned to their beds, after Sheriff Blount called out importantly that he had everything under control.

The Senior's office, built into a rear corner of the bank, had no outside door and only a single window. Its only entrance lay through the bank itself, and the Senior never let the one set of bank keys out of his possession. The window, heavily barred, blinded with a thick drape, was too high to be reached from outside without a ladder.

He heard a group of men tramping up the street. The Bearcat took on a burst of noise, most of the group crowding into the barroom. It didn't displease him, for it meant they had done their job. They spent in the Bearcat hangout a large part of the money he paid them, when in town, and he privately owned the Bearcat.

Some footsteps passed on by the bank and clumped on wooden stairs, heavily and slowly. He listened, frowning. Three or four men were carrying or dragging another up the steps to the jail above the sheriff's office next door. They halted. An iron door clanged shut. The men came down and crossed over to the saloon.

A pebble lightly struck the raised window. The Senior rose from his chair and pushed aside the thick drape. He frowned down at Zeigler, standing below in the side alley.

"Well?"

"We got the redhead," Zeigler reported. "He's in the jail now."

"Why didn't you kill him?"

"Thought sure we had, till we lit lamps an' saw he was trying to get up. I was about to finish him, but Blount wouldn't have it. Went sheriff, the way he still does at times. Something oughta be done about him."

"Something will, at the right time. But what about that other one—Bishop?"

Zeigler twitched a shoulder. "No sign of him. The redhead says they split up an' he came back by hisself. Blount got that out of him, me hitting him a coupla whacks. Then he passed out cold."

"You think he told the truth?"

"Looks that way."

Dissatisfied, the Senior shook his head. "He might have been lying, to give Bishop his chance. You tell Blount from me to stay close to the jail. And you keep the men sober. That's an order."

"Got it. Anything else?"

"Yes. I don't like your work lately."

Zeigler sucked in his thin lips, lowered his gaze from the shadowed face at the barred window, and stood mute. He knew too much to be fired off his job. The Senior's obsession with secrecy and personal security required a lonely grave for a trusted hireling who failed.

"Where's my son?" the Senior asked.

"He left soon after we broke into the house," Zeigler answered, relieved to change the subject. "He took the girl with him. His wife, I mean. She fought like a wildcat till we tied an' gagged her. She was still kicking when we put her in his buckboard behind the house."

"Did he say where he's taking her?"

"The Riverside Trading Post. He'll tame her there, he said." Aware that the trading post was Keller property, and that nobody there would dispute young Mansell's actions, Zeigler added, "I reckon he will, too!"

The Senior nodded agreement and approval. Mansell frequently irritated him with his dandyish airs, but he was sure that no son of his would lack mettle when called upon to assert his manhood in a domestic problem.

"How is Miss Blue?"

"Tied an' gagged in her bed upstairs. Blount don't know that. He'll find out, though, an' go sheriff on us. When do we turn her loose? I don't look forward to it. She's another wildcat. I hate tangling with women."

The Senior stroked his chin musingly. "Do you suppose the redhead might have set fire to the house before you caught him? To cover what he hoped would be his getaway?"

"No. We'd have seen it."

"Not if he was careful. Half an inch of lighted candle, on a blanket soaked in coal oil. Under the back porch, say, hidden from sight?"

"But he didn't go round to—"

"He might have," the Senior persisted. "Nobody's to swear he didn't. I'll not blame you if the house catches on fire and burns to the ground, with Miss Blue in it. In fact, I'd overlook your recent failures."

Zeigler stared up at him. His pale eyes widened. The oblique proposition appalled him. "Godamighty!" he breathed. "Be hell to pay if it got known!"

"So do it yourself and don't let anybody know," the Senior said bluntly. "You'll get a bonus. I always pay extra for special work, as you know."

"Special! This is—"

"Do it, or you're through. Understand? Through!" The window slid shut and the thick drape closed over it.

Moving out slowly from the alley, Zeigler tried to make a cigarette. His hands shook. He looked bitterly at the Bearcat Saloon, peopled by a dozen men, hardcases who took orders from him as their ramrod. The same men, at a word from the Senior, wouldn't hesitate to turn on him, hunt him down if he fled, execute him. He wasn't popular, and wearing the badge of a deputy sheriff didn't help, although they knew it was only a matter of convenience. Nobody trusted a renegade lawman.

His gaze switched to the big white house down the street, but avoided the faintly lighted window of the upstairs bedroom where Bonny Belle Blue lay trussed and gagged. He waited a minute, fearful of the task to be done, then went in search of a stub of candle, a blanket, and a can of coal oil.

# XIII

In the dark gap between the emporium and the saddle shop, Bishop meditated on what move lay open to him, if any. He chewed hard on his unlighted cigar. It didn't bring any inspiration worth developing, only increased his thirst and his dislike of the men preventing him from patronizing the Bearcat's barroom.

Having scouted the town the best he could without revealing himself, he concluded that the worst had happened, or the next worst to it. No telling what had become of Shamrock. Bonny might or might not be in her house. It was questionable, the house so silent. She was unconscious, perhaps. Or dead. As for Red Mackenzie, his case was relatively simple. Bishop had seen him hauled to jail.

His brief meditation couldn't discover for Bishop any weak spot in the set-up, much less evolve the rudiments of any sort of plan. The wakeful men in the Bearcat, and the bank's bright lantern, formed a tight safeguard on the jail. It looked bad for Red.

Remembering that the second-floor jail had an open gallery around it to provide entrance to the cells, Bishop carried his saddle rope coiled over his shoulder, with dwindling prospects of finding a use for it. His thoughts dwelt chiefly on Keller, on the baffling problem of locating Keller's whereabouts. The bank? At this hour? Well, maybe. No doubt Keller was up, keeping track of events.

He withdrew from the empty gap and passed on around the warehouse behind the emporium. The light from the street placed the buildings of the Keller Block in black silhouette, knife-edged angles and flat planes casting jumbled shadows. He saw the jail, stark above the shadows, and part of its gallery and railing. A rocking chair on the gallery struck an incongruously homey note.

Sheriff Blount appeared, ascending the stairway from his office. Pipe in mouth, the sheriff leisurely rounded the gallery and hit a cell door a perfunctory kick to test it. He made to return down the stairs, but evidently the cool night air won favor over his stuffy office. He lingered, shoving back his hat, then sat in the chair, lighted his pipe, and commenced rocking. Plainly, he was there to stay for a while.

So much for that. Bishop prowled in closer to the bank, losing sight of the sheriff. He heard low voices as he drew nearer. At the rear end of the alley alongside the bank, he froze, spying the speakers, one in the alley and the other behind an iron-barred window.

The conversation ceased. The window slid shut and a drawn drape blacked out its light. The man in the alley drifted off to the street, where he idled for a minute before shifting on.

Recognizing the man as Zeigler, Bishop eyed the barred window, guessing at the identity of the one behind it, wishing he could have overheard the private confab between Keller and his crew boss. It might have given him a pointer toward what action to take. He glared at the window.

Action. Any action was better than none. This thing couldn't be made much tougher to crack. Impatient, he moved along past the bank to behind the sheriff's office and scanned the jail above. There wasn't anything to rope onto. The monotonous creak of the rocking chair offended his ears. He despised rockers.

He took out his knife, paid thought to it, sheathed it again. Nothing to be gained by skewering the sheriff with a long throw up there. No help in getting onto the gallery. Difficult to score a hit, anyway. A miss, and the sheriff would bawl bloody murder. Bishop fingered his rope. Not long enough.

His impatience spilled over. Damn it, if he couldn't get to the sheriff, he'd get the sheriff to come to him. "Hey!" he called up, pitching his voice to a minor key. "Sheriff!"

The rocking chair gave a final creak. Footsteps sounded on the gallery, stopping at the door of the locked cell. "Well, what d'you want?"

"Me? Now you mention it, I want the hell out of this hole. Got the key? Kindly oblige—"

"Fat chance, joker! You called me for that?"

"I didn't call you."

"Somebody did."

"Sheriff!" Bishop repeated softly, flat against the back wall of the building.

Sheriff Blount loomed up at the railing, moving along it, leaning over to peer down into the darkness. "Who's there? You, Zeigler? Why the—"

He jerked back with a startled grunt, Bishop's loop settling on his shoulders. The loop snapped tight around his neck. Hauled forward off-balance in a low bow, hitting the top rail with his chin, he clawed at the strangling noose. The taut rope held him snared hard against the railing, on his knees, choking the life out of him. His frantic struggling weakened.

Bishop went up the rope hand over hand to the gallery and removed the noose. The sheriff lay crumpled, face purple and mouth open, air rasping in his throat. He would be a limp man for some time. Bishop took his keys and gun from him.

At the door of the locked cell, he muttered, "This the right address of a crippled Caledonian?"

"Sweet St. Andrew!" Red breathed. "You!"

"Who did you expect? Mary Queen of Scots?"

"Watch out for the sheriff. He was here only a—"

"Never mind the sheriff. He's catching his breath. How bad are you damaged?"

"Clubbed, creased, booted and stepped on, but not crippled."

"This'll help ease your aches." Bishop thrust the keys and gun at Red through the bars. "You can reach the lock from inside. I don't have time to find the right key. You'll have to pick up a horse. My black kicked the dun and it broke for home, wherever that is. There's a bunch of horses outside the Bearcat."

"And a bunch of guns inside!" Red said.

"That reminds me. Rustle another gun and spare shells from the sheriff's office when you go through."

"Just like that! Why can't I climb down off the gallery? You've got a rope."

"Yeah, and I've got my own use for it."

On the south side of the jail, the gallery abutted the flat roof of the bank, which was edged by a foot of firewall and the higher rise of ornamental false-front. Southwestern fashion, the firewall was pierced at intervals by *canales,* narrow slots, spouted to run off water in the rare event of rainstorms. On lonely *ranchos* they also served as rifle-slots when under Indian attack.

Crouching to allow the false-front to shield him from the street, Bishop crept over the roof to the far side of the bank and looked down into the alley. He was directly above the barred window of Keller's office. His roping trick on the sheriff was worth trying once more, though it stretched luck and would have to be played in reverse. Reverse, he reflected, was the right word for it.

But nowhere to fasten the rope to bear his weight. He made a return trip to the jail gallery, wrenched the sheriff's rocking chair apart with as little noise as possible, and took three of its rungs back. He lashed onto the rungs with a bight of the rope, leaving both ends of the rope free.

He had to work quickly, no time for safe-checking. Red Mackenzie shouldn't take long to quit the jail and go through the sheriff's office, then grab a horse for his getaway. It was unlikely that he could do it without a rumpus. A miracle.

Bishop jammed the three tied rungs crosswise against the slot of a *canale*. The running noose he slipped over his left ankle. He eased over the firewall head first, using the other part of the rope to lower himself, and hung upsidedown, his face level with the upper sash of Keller's window. It struck him then that he had maneuvered into a damnably precarious position. He was a dangling duck for any man's bullet. The risk, he told himself, was justified. He couldn't think of any other way to get at Keller.

He snapped a finger on the window pane.

Light broke through, the thick drape brushed aside. The bottom sash slid up.

"Well?"

Bishop hung waiting, a giant bat, unmoving. A predator poised for prey. As yet he could see only a hand holding back the drape beneath him.

Keller's face came to the opened window. "Well? Damn it, Zeigler, stand where I can see you! Is the job done?"

Two large and muscular hands flashed in between the iron bars. Their fingers clamped on his neck. Keller stared horrified into baleful, upside-down eyes. He tried to scream for help. The fingers squeezed his windpipe shut. All he could get out was a gurgle, sticking in his throat, before that too was shut off.

He tore at the gripping hands, at the wrists, futilely. They stayed as rigid as the iron bars of the window. He kept on struggling, his efforts growing feebler. A last

spasm twitched his body taut and spent itself. His head
lolled, mouth agape, tongue protruding. Bishop hoisted
him up close to the bars. He changed his grip, releasing
one hand to search Keller's pockets.

Wearing two gunbelts, Red Mackenzie felt his way
to the door of the sheriff's office and gentled it open a
crack. Urgency fought caution. Ransacking the office in
pitch darkness had taken time. It had cost long minutes
to find the sheriff's armory of firearms, locked in a wall
cabinet, and a minute more to fit the right key into the
padlock.

He ranged an estimating eye along the line of horses
at the Bearcat hitchrack, picking in advance a sorrel
as the likeliest-looking animal of the lot for his getaway.
The sorrel had size, good lines, powerful hindquarters.
Its saddle dished shallowly to a low cantle, the kind
Red happened to prefer. The stirrups were let out at
about his length. He got ready to make for the sorrel.

A man came to the Bearcat's swingdoors and looked
out over them toward the sheriff's office and jail. Red
swore under his breath. Another delay. Time crawled.
Somebody in the barroom spoke to the man, who nodded
response, putting his back to the swingdoors and hook-
ing both elbows over them. The one who had spoken to
him went on talking, the man presently shaking his head
and saying something in argument. Red edged out of the
sheriff's office and turned right to cross the street farther
up, away from the light.

"Took you long enough!" came a whisper, and suddenly he found Bishop was behind him.

Where Bishop had emerged from, Red didn't inquire.
"I lost time looking for—"

"Long enough for me to do what I wanted!"

"Find out anything about Shamrock?"

"No." Bishop held a gun lined on the back-turned man at the Bearcat. "Mosey on!"

"Where's your horse?"

"In a brush patch off beyond the cottonwoods. Get one of your own!"

"Watch me do that!"

A hoarse cry halted Red's first stride. The cry rose to the thin note of a scream, pinched and quivering with pain, rage, shattered nerves.

"Holy saints, a woman's getting killed!"

Bishop flipped out his second gun. "No, it's Keller getting alive. I should've made sure of him." The reason he hadn't was reluctance to commit plain murder; the reluctance of a gunfighter who followed the rules. He heard heavy gruntings and flounderings overhead on the jail gallery. "Him and the sheriff. Run for a horse!"

Keller's nightmarish screech had stilled all sound in the Bearcat, for the few instants it lasted. It changed, became more recognizably the voice of a furious man uttering broken words. The sheriff, not yet finding his voice, hammered a fist on the floor of the gallery.

Chairs and boots banged. The man at the swingdoors whirled, flinging the doors wide and snatching at his holster. Sprinting across Bishop's line of fire, Red slung a low shot. The man tumbled onto one knee, shouting, "Goddam redhead—he's broke jail!"

Shadows swarmed along the barroom windows, and Bishop headed for the alley. Somebody cracked a hasty shot at him as he passed into the full glare of the bank's lantern. Men were pouring now from the Bearcat. The shot, and two more after it, missed, which surprised Bishop; then he realized that the bright light dazzled the shooters' eyes, and he stopped directly beneath the lantern.

Keller's yelling grew more coherent, calling out from his office window in the alley. No doubt he kept a gun in his office, probably a shotgun, which made the alley a poor route for a getaway. The sheriff regained his voice, loudly complaining he'd been robbed of his keys and gun.

"—And Mackenzie's gone!"

Red Mackenzie wasn't gone. His going had stalled on an obstacle: the sorrel. The sorrel's owner had perhaps trained it to be a one-man horse and it knew Red was not its man. Or else it possessed an unruly disposition, aggravated by the gunshots. As soon as Red freed its rein and legged into the saddle, the sorrel humped its back and threw a jarring bone-shaker to buck him off.

Red stayed on, his right toe fishing for the flapping stirrup. He had picked the wrong horse, but now it was too late to swap for another. He was stuck with it, the rest of the hitched horses rearing and kicking, the Bearcat men taking potshots at him. The sorrel hung its head and launched a series of twisting jumps, high-rollers, trying to shake him off. Red leaned low over the lee side, hanging on by one leg and arm, Indian warrior fashion, to keep his fractious mount between himself and the shooters, but the sorrel then changed ends and took to bucking in circles.

"He's on my horse!" a man rapped, running into the street. The muzzle of his gun followed the gyrating, bobbing target. "Leave him to me—I'll knock him off!" Horses plunging at the hitchrack snapped their tied reins and swirled between him and the sorrel, stamping up boils of dust.

"Watch where you're shooting! My horse—"

"*Watch out for Bishop!*"

"Where?"

"*There!*"

In the disk of shadow cast by the base of the big lantern Bishop stood motionless, partly obscured by the rising dust as well as by the blinding effect of the unshaded light overhead. The mica-laden dust, catching the light, formed a cloudy incandescence like billows of thin fog mirroring sunshine. Through it he could make out men erupting from the Bearcat, chasing the runaway horses, raising further dust and confusion.

He held his fire, thinking that the uproar might provide an opportunity for him to get to his hidden horse without a running fight on foot. There were too many shooters to take on, more than he had estimated. Keller evidently had undercover connections, sources that promptly supplied additional hardcases when needed. His secret operations were known among close-mouthed riders of the chaparral.

It was up to Red to straighten out the sorrel and be on his way, before they shot him to rags. "Get a move on," Bishop muttered, meaning himself, and took a pace for experiment.

At once, his movement drew attention. A bullet smacked the front of the bank. He rapidly calculated how long it must take him to run the gauntlet of the lighted area before him. Too long. A stark target in a hail of lead. He fired straight up at the lantern's wide base. The lantern merely swung an inch. Its base was steel.

Down at the south end of the street a red glow flickered behind tall windows. Red against white. A tinkle of glass was what caused Bishop to glance toward the white house. His deepset eyes widened, staring aghast.

From a broken upstairs window poked a gagged face, yellow-gold hair in disarray, smoke gushing out above it. The fact that she was gagged, and that her arms weren't visible, meant that Bonny was tied, probably bound hand and foot. She had managed to roll to the window and break it open for air, but there she was trapped, unable even to call for help.

The red glow flickered brighter. A ball of flame burst up at the rear of the house.

On the jail gallery, Sheriff Blount shouted, "House on fire! Get buckets, you men!"

"Get 'em y'self!" retorted a man from the Bearcat. "It ain't our business."

"Buckets!" the sheriff repeated. "Water! It's the Blue woman's house."

"A blue woman?" someone jeered. "I never seen one."

"Miss Blue—she's—"

"Aw, shut it off! We're here for blood, not water!"

## XIV

Bishop spat an oath. Baleful wrath replaced his dismay. He was guilty of many transgressions, but none that touched this hideous deed of deliberately burning a woman alive. His wrath spread to include not only Keller but all of Keller's hirelings. These men were the bottom scrapings of the gunmen breed.

"Hell perish 'em!"

He gave no further calculation to running the gauntlet. His getaway faded to trifling insignificance. Attack. Smash the enemy, then snatch poor doomed Bonny out of that holocaust. In that order. Fast. It had to be fast.

His heavy guns kicked alive, a shattering roar of rapid fire that shocked into silence the guns across the street. A man faltered in mid-stride, hit, pointing an arm vaguely at the tall dark figure under the bank's lantern, at the spurting flashes, as if mutely demanding vengeance. He was the owner of the sorrel. The stunned reaction cracked. Forsaking him, others dived to earth.

Firing low, Bishop automatically kept count of his shots. Twelve shots summed the limit of his attack. No time to reload. He was icily calm now, professionalism taking over from the moment of wild wrath.

At his eleventh shot the men broke scrambling for better cover, firing back into the dusty haze. One stood his ground, legs straddled bent-kneed, crouched on the boardwalk before the Bearcat. He wore his hair long, and his hat was round-crowned, no crease. An Indian or halfbreed; or a white renegade imbued with Indian bravado.

"Just one of him, ain't there?" he snarled, trying to

rally support. "Just one! What if he *is* Bishop? He's just a—" Bishop's last bullet clipped his right shoulder. "Son of a bitch!" he said, heading for the barroom.

The sorrel was throwing fits worse than ever, Red taking the bumps—a good rider on a good horse, but not on good terms with each other. Bishop ran and leaped at its head, which didn't do anything toward gentling its temper. He got his arm around its neck and a hand-hold on an ear, hauling it down from a high buck, using brute strength and some punishment that entailed ear-twisting. Considerably impressed, the snorting sorrel barged down the street, Red in the saddle, Bishop hanging on alongside.

Abreast of the white house Bishop dropped off. Bonny was leaning precariously far out through the broken window, wrists tied behind her, prepared to topple out and break her neck rather than burn to death.

"Hold on, Bonny!" Bishop called up to her. She rolled her head, either in assent or warning, he couldn't tell which.

Red, jumping from the saddle, snubbed the reins up short. The sorrel stood trembling, subdued. Men appeared in the street, casting long shadows, the light of the bank's lantern behind them, making dark silhouettes of them.

"Stand 'em off till I come out, Red!"

Sheer optimism. Getting into the burning house was simple, but getting out alive was a different matter. And for one man to stand off an armed mob . . . "Then what?" came Red's ironic query.

"Then stand 'em off some more—my guns are empty."

Bishop ran to the front door, arm outstretched to fling it open. The door opened ahead of his touch and he nearly collided into Zeigler, coming out gun in hand. Zeigler had done a thorough job of the task assigned to him, making certain by setting fires within the house as well as outside.

For an instant the two men stared into each other's eyes. Neither of them changed expression, both being masters of violence, constantly alert, never affording to betray a hint of surprise, of unpreparedness. Bishop, empty guns in his holsters, stabbed his right hand at Zeigler's gun as it whipped up, and batted it higher.

The gun exploded a shell at the ceiling. Bishop feinted another stab at it, struck Zeigler in the mouth, and followed through with his left fist. Zeigler's head snapped back. The next blow tottered him on his heels to a fall. Blinking at such bruiser tactics on the part of a noted gunfighter, he tried for a shot from the floor.

Bishop booted the gun from his hand. He bent and hauled Zeigler up. Fire was eating through a wall, lighting the hallway. It etched saturnine lines in his face. He turned a glittering stare to it, and then to Zeigler.

"You like fire?"

Zeigler cracked, reading the intention in the angrily merciless eyes. "Don't, man! No!" His split and bleeding lips gaped. "Don't, for—"

"Fire you'll have!" said Bishop.

He raised the squirming body and heaved it full force from him. Zeigler vanished. The burning patch of wall became a ragged hole belching sparks from the room beyond. Outside, Red's guns began thudding.

The rear wall of the living room was ablaze, and a doorway in it showed the adjoining back parlor to be a mass of flame, crackling, hissing, devouring Bonny's fine belongings. Curtains swayed in the gusts of heated air. Not for long. The house was going up like matchwood.

Bishop went up the staircase in leaps to the second

floor, shouting for Bonny, unsure which room she was in. Here the smoke gathered so thickly he had to feel his way from room to room, smashing windows to let it out and release some of the oven-like heat.

A locked door balked him. He pounded on it, and heard a voice, faint in the increasing roar of fire. He backed off and rammed his foot at the door. It held fast. Cursing behind closed lips, his eyes and nose stinging, he drove at it with his shoulder and crashed it in.

A corner of the room had burned through, creating a scorching air-draft between it and the broken window. The floor was buckling, fire below warping its timbers. On his hands and knees Bishop found the smoke less thick, the air draft sucking it up. Crawling to Bonny, huddled low at the window, he knifed off her ropes and gag, cursing again to himself. The ropes had been tied brutally tight.

"Can you use your legs?"

"Sure!" she gasped, but stiffened muscles belied her when she tried, letting her sink helplessly against him. "Help me out the window."

"Hell with that!"

"Rogue, I'm—"

"Hold your breath."

He slung her onto his shoulder. She made a lighter load than he would have judged, but to crawl while carrying her was out of the question. Too awkward, too slow, and the floor growing intolerably hot, about to flare up at any minute. He rose and bore her to the door.

The upstairs passage was a tunnel of dense smoke, tinged red, dimly penetrated by a glare at the far end. Stooped, Bishop plunged through it, holding his breath, trusting that Bonny was doing the same. A prolonged crash shook the house, part of the rear roof collapsing, and the change of draft thinned the smoke, drawing it off in the rush of heat. The staircase looked like a chute into a furnace.

Fire had spread along a side wall of the living room and reached the front hallway. Draperies and tapestries bloomed blackened streaks, flamed, fell in burning shreds, Bishop heard Bonny husk from her parched throat, "My God, we'll roast!"

Her blue velvet cloak hung over the banister of the staircase, like a Spanish shawl. The gorgeous garment was getting old, but she, with her love of vivid color, couldn't bring herself to discard it. She liked to hang it where she could see its brilliant turquoise hue and rich texture. Even now, hoping to save it, she pulled it off the banister.

Bishop took the cloak from her and bundled her in it to shield her inflammable hair and dress. Carrying her slung on his back like a swag in a blanket, disregarding her muffled protests that she couldn't see where she was going, he descended the stairs to the living room. The arched entrance of the hallway was a flaming horseshoe.

Sidling along the front wall, he tugged down the broad brim of his hat, turned up his coat collar, hunched his shoulders. It was just as well Bonny couldn't see where she was going.

He charged head-down at the hallway. Intense heat enveloped him. His boot-heels punched into charred floorboards. Then he was hurtling out of the front door, trailing sparks, Bonny bumping on his back.

Red Mackenzie, holding onto the scaredly dancing sorrel while aiming a shot up the street, spared a quick look at him. "I about gave you up!"

Townsmen, half-dressed, were demanding to know the whyfor of the shooting when a house was burning down. Keller could be heard calling for Zeigler. Several townsmen of action, attempting to organize a bucket brigade, clogged the purposes of the men from the Bearcat, getting in their way. Others argued discouragingly that the house was a total loss; let it burn out. Not worth risking a bullet from the lunatic who was taking pot-shots at all comers.

"Get that redhead!" shouted Sheriff Blount. "There goes Bishop!"

Bishop gulped fresh air and wiped his streaming eyes. The skin of his face felt seared. "Stand 'em off another minute, can you? Give me time to—"

"Can try," Red said. "A minute at most. Sheriff's got the town with him." He couldn't have imagined ever seeing the coolly self-possessed Rogue Bishop in so deplorable a condition, face smoke-blackened, eyes glazed, bloodshot, his voice a dry croak. But he said nothing about that. He didn't think Bishop would appreciate it.

Not pausing to unwrap Bonny or inquire the state of her heath, Bishop hurried on to the covering darkness of the cottonwoods.

Hidden in the brush beyond the cottonwoods, the black horse snuffled uneasily, disliking the smoky odor that its owner brought with him, and rolling an eye at the blueclad bundle. There at last Bishop unloaded Bonny. Leaving her to untangle herself, he stretched on the ground, breathing deeply, rubbing his shoulder.

"Canteen on my saddle."

They drank tepid water from the canteen. Bonny combed her hair with her fingers, straightened her rumpled dress, shook out the cloak. "What's wrong with your shoulder? Bullet?"

"No. Damn near dislocated it on your bedroom door."

"The door was made to open out, not in."

"Accounts for it." He reloaded his guns. "Your next house, make sure the doors don't open that way. Makes trouble for a man getting to you."

"Tough," Bonny said, massaging her ankles. She knew better than to try thanking him for what he had done. "Is stale water all you can offer to a lady?"

"Flask in my saddle pocket."

She got it, sipped raw spirits, and passed it to him. "What did they do with Shamrock?" Bishop asked.

Before Bonny could reply, a horseman rounded the patch of brush and stamped to a standstill. "Bishop?"

"This way, Red."

Red pushed into the brush and dismounted, looking at Bishop and Bonny resting on the ground, the flask between them. A dirty pink halo of smoke hung high overhead, crowning sullenly the noise-filled town. "Cozy," he commented, tartly ironic. "Mind if I join the party?"

"Help yourself."

"Thanks." He picked up the flask and took a swallow. "I had to stand off a volunteer fire brigade of townsmen. From the shouting, seems I'm the one who set the house afire, and you kidnaped Miss Bonny. We're loaded with crimes!"

"I'm no kid," Bonny said, "but if this is napping I won't lay any charges. You through with that flask?"

Red handed it to her. "The Bearcat boys are catching up their horses to come after us. Just thought I'd mention it."

"You're a cool customer."

"I'm hot inside. When I skipped out, Keller—guess it was him—was calling to somebody to fetch him his horse. He sounded like a hardnose colonel. Where's Shamrock? In Keller's house?"

"No, she's—"

"Never mind that now," Bishop broke in, rising. "Bonny, you'll have to ride up behind me." He swung into the saddle and helped her on. "Where to?"

"Do you know the Riverside Trading Post?"

"You don't mean Shamrock's there!"

"I'm afraid I do, Rogue."

"God Almighty!" Red muttered, and Bishop's lips flattened hard.

They cleared out of the brush and veered onto the southbound road. Bonny, perched none too easily behind Bishop, her blue cloak fluttering, looked back, sighing.

"There goes my grand big house, all my lovely treasures, my fine clothes—everything!"

"Forget it."

"Rogue, I'm woozy. Lightheaded. It's not the liquor."

"I know. You'll get over it. You were drugged, I'm pretty sure. That wasn't any heart attack. You've got a heart like a horse. Did Shamrock tell you you were laid out for dead?"

"Yes. Told me the pills were gone. The pills that old quack gave me, to make me sleep. It couldn't have been anybody but the Senior who slipped them to me. Keller! In my wine. Tried to put me to sleep for good. The murdering hypocrite! The—"

"About Shamrock," Red put in, riding close abreast on the sorrel. "Get to her! What happened?"

Bonny rounded her eyes at him. "Woo-hoo! Listen and learn. Zeigler and some others got inside the house while Shamrock was busy drowning me with black coffee. After they grabbed her, Junior came in. Young Mansell. I could kill him! His father, too! How they fooled me! Me—Bonny Belle Blue—the terror of flimflam artists and cardsharks!"

"Did they hurt her?"

"They didn't do her any good. Junior told them to tie her in his buckboard behind the house, and do it quiet. Gag her. Which they did. I was groggy, but I knew what was going on. All that black coffee. I heard Junior tell Zeigler to let his father know where he was going with her. The Riverside Trading Post. He spoke like his father owns it, or owns an interest in it. You can guess why he took her there, Rogue."

"Aims to tame his unwilling bride," Bishop commented "in a place that's safe from interference."

"It's my fault!" Bonny grieved. "I steered her into marrying him, so she'd be set up as a real lady, respected by the best people. Upper crust. Class."

"With a share of it shining on yourself, eh? Women!"

"I hate to admit it, but it's true. I can see that now. Poor kid, she only married him to please me. Unwilling bride is right! She told me how she tongue-lashed him after the wedding. Belittled him to his face. Made a monkey of him in front of everybody. He'll never forgive her! He'll take it out on her! My fault—I let her in for it!"

"Dry your tears!" Bishop commanded harshly over his shoulder. "You talk like young Keller's an imp from hell!"

"It's a hell-hole he's taken her to!" Bonny retorted. "You should've seen the look on his face when they tied up Shamrock and carried her out to his buckboard! What he'll do to her, Piety folks—ordinary folks—wouldn't stand for, hearing her screaming. *That's* why he took her off to the Riverside hell-hole. No other reason, is there? *Is* there?"

"Can't think of one, offhand. Unless he likes the stink of it. Stank like a coyote den, last time I was there."

"How much do screams matter in that place?"

"Damn little."

"A girl's screams?"

"No difference. Everybody minds his own business."

"God Almighty!" Red muttered again. "Can we get in there, Bishop?"

"Can try."

"With the Keller posse after us?" Bonny questioned. "They must know where we're going now—know I heard Junior say where he's taken Shamrock."

"So we outride 'em. Maybe by thirty minutes. They got a late start, catching their horses." Bishop heeled the black to a stretching run. "Hold on tight, Bonny!"

"Thirty minutes! How do you bust the Riverside in thirty minutes? It's stockaded and guarded like Bent's Fort!"

"Can try."

## XV

Bishop had some past acquaintance with the Riverside
Trading Post, and Red Mackenzie knew of it from hear-
say, as did Bonny. Its reputation exceeded its importance as a commercial establishment.

Originally a Mexican settlement on the old Cananea
Trail, where the trail met the fording of Whitewater
Wash over to Mexico, and then abandoned, it had
since changed ownership several times. Now it was
solid, compactly rebuilt to serve as a roadhouse, a stop-
over for rustlers and smugglers, a lodge for hunted men
able to pay for a hideout. A profitable enterprise.

The law couldn't dent it. Maintaining a gun-crew to
man its enclosing stockade, the self-styled trading post
defied investigation, beat off occasional Apache raids,
and preserved business terms with bandits who came
up over the river bearing loot to trade.

The main building, high on the riverbank, bastioned
the south side of the yard. Once the adobe church of the
Mexican settlement, crude wings had since been added
to it and a second floor of chinked logs built on, making
an unlovely landmark that could be seen for miles in clear
air. It housed the barroom and hotel accommodations,
kitchen, eating room, store. Paying guests could relax in
rough comfort and sleep at night with both eyes shut.

Having put up at the Riverside Trading Post a time
or two, Bishop ran over in his mind the lay of it, the
crew's bunkhouse, the horse corral and tack shed, and
the ruins of adobe cabins. There was the main building,
blocking up above the pointed-log stockade fence. Its
second floor of sleeping rooms, musty cubbyholes he

recalled, jutted out over the sheer riverbank. Props supported it from sagging. A piece of clumsy carpentering, but effectively preventing anyone from climbing in.

From the shortening distance he surveyed the place, seeking a possible entrance. The stockade, no. Prowling Apaches had tried it and, shot by lookouts, died impaled on those sharp-tipped logs. Lights in the yard. The stockade gate, wide to allow wagons to pass through, hung open, which meant that men were up and about, although day as yet was only a pale rumor in the eastern sky.

It had to be the gate. Bishop raised a hand for Red to slow down. "We ride up easy, but not too easy. They'll see our horses are lathered. They'll know we didn't dawdle. But swoop in on 'em, they'll knock us off before we reach the gate."

"Reminds me of a *bandido fortaleza* down in Durango. Here on U. S. territory! Must have some powerful connections."

"Keller, for one. Among other things it's a rendezvous for dodgers, gunhands, army deserters and the like. A kind of recruiting station for those who qualify. They make contacts here. Some of the contacts are big men. Like Keller. Drop off, Bonny. We'll pick you up after—"

"Drop off, my eye!" Bonny interrupted. "That hell-hole can't show me anything I haven't seen before! I'm going in with you—I owe it to Shamrock."

Bishop shrugged, not making an issue of it. Bonny's presence might prove helpful, at that. It ought to smother suspicion, two riders accompanied by a woman, though that depended on what Mansell Keller had said when he arrived with his trussed bride in the buckboard.

"Okay, Bonny. Don't talk. Don't show surprise at anything you see or hear. Nor you, Red. Act casual. I'll do the talking."

"What'll you talk about?" Red asked.

"The weather. It's a safe subject."

"Oh, sure! 'Good morning, folks, don't shoot us, we're only here to bust—' "

"Don't talk, I said!"

"Beg pardon, m'lord!"

The open gate of the stockade allowed a cross-section view of the yard and part of the bunkhouse. Two men with rifles stepped out into the gateway, one from each side. The approach of the horses had been heard, but Bishop sent forward a hail for the sake of common custom.

"Halloo, the house!"

It earned a beckoning gesture from one of the two gate guards. They rested their rifles, but stayed where they stood.

"Howdy," Bishop greeted when he and Red reined in before them for inspection. He didn't know them. New hands. "Another hot day coming up. We'll be riding back to Piety in the heat, dammit."

"You come from Piety?"

"Yeah. Is Laborde still here?"

"He sure is." The pair moved aside, scanning Bonny with lively interest. Four men had emerged from the bunkhouse and were watching. One of the guards called to them, "It's okay." Eyes on Bonny, he said, perking his lips, "Make yourselves to home. I bet Laborde'll be pleased to see you."

Bishop turned toward the main building. "This way to the barroom, Red."

"Will it be open at this hour?"

"It's open round the clock. They don't keep ordinary hours here. The night trade comes in rushes, generally from Mexico. Then it can get noisy."

"Who's Laborde?" Bonny asked. "I seem to remember that name from some years back. Gambler?"

"No. Laborde's the head man, the manager. Calls

himself the 'factor'—he's French-Canadian. Skipped Canada with a pile of cash belonging to the Hudson's Bay Company. Got whipsawed out of it in a sky-high faro game. Never gambled since."

"What's he look like?"

"Like a living skeleton. Big feller, tall as me, but skin and bones. Dark. Wears his hair long. He's got an eye for a pretty woman, so watch your step when you meet him."

Bonny clapped a hand to her brow. "We've met! It's him! There couldn't be two like him. I can tell you where and when he dropped his wad."

"Tombstone?"

"Yes. In the Blue Palace, same week I sold it. Some of the fast boys wanted to buy me out, but couldn't meet my price. Along came this Canuck, a creepy big spook, loaded with British gold. The boys rigged a teaser, letting him spot the run of the cards. He plunged, thinking he couldn't lose. A no-limit game."

"Then," Bishop guessed, "they switched boxes and fed him a cold deck."

"Broke him," Bonny confirmed.

"I s'pose he saw you there. Would he remember you?"

"Saw me? I'll say he did! What's more, he saw me banking his British gold after the boys bought my Blue Palace!"

"Bishop," said Red, "I think we're getting our tails caught in a crack! Your Canuck friend won't welcome Miss Bonny with any loving kindness."

Dismounting, Bishop tied his horse up to a hitchrack. "If I'd known about that, I wouldn't have let her come in with us. Damned bad enough as it was. Laborde's no friend of mine. Well—might as well see it through, now we're here."

"Nothing much else for it, is there?"

"Not unless we run for the gate."

"That, sir, doesn't strike my fancy," Red said. The two gate guards were watching them. So were the men outside the bunkhouse. But what Red was mainly concerned about, Bishop surmised, was Shamrock. Shamrock O'Terran Keller, another man's lawfully wedded wife.

It occurred to Bishop that a question of morals was involved in the situation. Strictly on the face of it, and disregarding the circumstances, did a man have a moral right to snatch an unhappy bride away from her husband? An awkward question, complicated by foreseeable awkward consequences if the snatching succeeded. He dismissed it from his mind. Too many other problems to tackle.

In the quiet barroom two men looked up from a makeshift checkerboard inked on the table between them, glanced at Bishop and Red, and shuttled their regard to Bonny. At another table a solitaire player smeared his layout and leaned back to roll a cigarette, grunting, "Hi," to the three newcomers.

"Hi," Bishop returned, putting him down as a bored guest, a dodger gone into hiding. The checker players belonged here, marked by the rifle that each kept lying on the floor close by his chair. A state of alertness ruled the Riverside Trading Post at all times. Laborde imposed a semi-military discipline on his crew, banishing penniless and unarmed any man he found slacking off.

The barroom, transformed from the Mexican church, had adobe walls, narrow windows, a tamped floor laid down by some working padre wise in the durable value of adobe mixed with a measure of ox-blood. A crudely built staircase occupied one end of it, leading through a hole in the ceiling to the rooms above. The stale air stank of burned lamp-oil and human sweat, with a leavening of strong liquor and unventilated tobacco fumes. Bonny twitched her nose, professionally disapproving of any dive that neglected reasonable cleanliness.

A sleepy barman, the only one on duty, nodded to Bishop, recognizing him, scanning curiously his smoke-grimed face and singed eyebrows. "What happened to you?" he inquired while setting out a bottle and glasses.

"Got scorched fighting a fire in Piety," Bishop told him. "Did Mansell Keller get here all right? I didn't see his buckboard in the yard."

"It's in the wagon shed. It broke down." The barman absently mopped the bar. "Junior ain't much of a driver, I guess. He side-swiped a gate post. Was in a rush. I had to ready a room fast, though that ain't my job." He leered upward at the ceiling. "His honeymoon."

"When did he—they—get here?"

"Not long ago. It was noisy up there for a while after he locked the door. Then I heard him unlock it."

Red's face grayed, rigid. Bonny bit her lip. "What room are they in?" Bishop asked.

"What d'you want to know for?"

"We've brought him a message. It's important."

The barman moved away. Leaving the bar, he spoke in a low tone to the checker players. One of them rose and left by a door at the far end from the staircase.

"Sent for Laborde," Bishop murmured.

Presently, Laborde entered the barroom. A big-boned man, tall and stoop-shouldered, he walked springily like a forest Indian, but his skin had a dead pallor and his body was gaunt as if consumed by a wasting disease. A cowl of black hair, cut straight above heavy-lidded eyes, accentuated the pallor. He levelled a piercing stare at Bonny, and halted, stockstill.

"Hello, *M'sieur le Facteur*," Bishop greeted him, in a flattering attempt to smooth Franco-American relations.

It wasn't much, but the best he could do on the spur of the moment. "How are you?"

Monsieur ignored the courteous gambit. His cadaverous face showed no expression whatever. "You bring a message from Piety? An important message for the son?" He kept his stare on Bonny, who fidgeted uneasily.

"That's right."

"Tell me the message. I will give it to him when he comes down. He is not now to be disturb'."

Bishop shook his head. "It's private and very urgent. "I," he lied barefaced, "am troubleshooting for Keller, your boss."

"What trouble?"

"That's private, too. If Keller wants you to know, he'll tell you. My job here is to see Junior, personally, never mind how much he's disturbed. Something's come up. An urgent family matter." Bishop's tone roughened. "Don't hinder me!"

Laborde transferred his stare from Bonny to Bishop. "I give the orders here!"

"You won't for long, if you cross Keller's orders!"

The staring eyes wavered slightly. At last Laborde said, "Upstairs. Second room at back." He thrust a bony finger at Bonny. "Not her! Leave her! She stays—"

"She goes with us," Bishop contradicted him. He paced to the staircase with Bonny and Red. There he glanced back to see how Laborde took it. Laborde was motioning to the same man who had summoned him from his office. The man hurried out of the barroom.

"Sent over to the bunkhouse for his crew. He's hell-bent on keeping you, Bonny!"

"Don't I know it! Those snaky eyes! But would he try it at gunpoint? Set the crew on us? Even though he thinks Keller sent us?"

"He's not altogether convinced of that. A wrong move, and we'll blow the works."

"How can we get Shamrock out?" Red muttered. "Past the crew, the yard, the gate . . . And the posse can't be far off by now."

Bishop shook his head. "One thing at a time. Tackle 'em as they come, is all I know."

"But how?

"Damned if I know that."

## XVI

The three of them climbed the stairs together to a cramped and bare-floored passage that, windowless, trapped the foul air rising from below. A crack of lamplight shone under the door of the second room at the back. They paused there to listen. The only sound from within was a faint moan.

Red reached for the doorknob. His eyes held murder. Bishop fended his hand off, fearing a mad reaction from him at what they might find. He twisted the doorknob quietly and inched the door inward. The faint moan came again. There was a sound of harsh breathing. Something scraped, like fingernails scratching on wood. Abruptly, Bishop pushed the door open.

The room was a shambles. Washstand, dresser, chair, everything it contained lay piled onto the overturned bed. He took in that much, before he jerked his head back from the downward swipe of a brass object that smacked the forebrim of his hat. "Damn!" He cuffed the hat up off his eyes, and rammed the door wide.

Shamrock jumped from behind it, shirt torn and hair disheveled. "Rogue!" she exclaimed. "Red! Bonny! How in the name of—"

"Quiet," Bishop hushed her. Red and Bonny pushed in behind him and shut the door. "Where's Junior? Keep your voice down—they're listening below."

"He's under the bed. He got right rough. I was bouncing all over the room, him clawing at me, me kicking him."

"Looks it. So do you. Your shirt's open."

Shamrock pulled her torn shirt together, smiling shame-

134

lessly at Red. "He cornered me by the washstand. In the tussle I slipped my wrists loose. Broke the pitcher on his head. Then I hit him with this." She wagged the brass candlestick in her right hand. "Then I tipped the bed over on top of him and buried him, in case he came to."

Red shook his head at her in wonder. "And I thought you needed taking care of! All the noise didn't bring up anybody, eh?"

"No. I unlocked the door, hoping—so I could whack him and take his gun, naturally."

"Naturally," said Red. "Hardcase with a gun. Girl with a candlestick. He wouldn't have a chance, Lord help him!"

Thoughtfully, Shamrock placed the brass candlestick on the piled furniture. Clasping her hands, she raised soft eyes and contrived to appear defenselessly feminine. "Oh, I was so desperately afraid until you showed up! Terrified!" Her voice broke. The tear in her shirt opened again. She didn't seem to be aware of it. "I wondered if I'd ever escape from this place!"

"You can go on wondering," Bishop told her. "For all of us. We're all desperate."

He lifted the covering wreckage off Junior to have a look at him. Junior lay moaning with each breath, his fingers digging spasmodically at the floor. What the pitcher had missed doing, the candlestick had accomplished, possibly aided further by the bedstead.

"Here's a pretty limp bridegroom," Bishop commented, to remind Shamrock that she was, after all, married. He was a little astonished at Shamrock's unusual behavior in suddenly becoming utterly feminine, unashamedly exerting captivating charm on Red Mackenzie. Especially with her legal spouse in the same room.

The reminder passed unheeded. Shamrock went on gazing at Red as if really seeing him for the first time, or as if he had changed into someone else. The strong current between them could be sensed. Bishop experienced a small twinge of envy, a feeling of loss, realizing that he was shut out, an outsider. In her young heart Shamrock had chosen him to replace her father and confused the attachment with love, and that was forever gone. She had outgrown it.

Red moved toward her, his arms spreading. Bonny slowly nodded her compassionate understanding. Youth to youth. Damn any man-made laws. To the vagrant wind with them. Young man, young woman. Natural affinity. Bonny spread her compassion to Bishop, particularly. Rogue Bishop was too old for Shamrock.

Not old in the ordinary counting of years, no. A most powerful, virile man. But aged and seasoned by experience. His kind aged fast. The graying hair came early over the temples. He was too old for a girl of nineteen, going on twenty. And the girl a virgin, as Bonny knew.

Somebody knocked on the door.

Red turned and braced his foot against the bottom of the door to bar it from opening. Bishop clapped a hand over Junior's moaning mouth. The knocking came again.

"Mr. Keller! You all right?" It was the barman's voice, grumblingly respectful to Keller's son. "Laborde sent me up to ask you—though it ain't my job."

Laborde had evidently taken second thought and grown more suspicious. And the barman must have used care to come up unheard, avoiding creaking floorboards, probably by Laborde's order. Bishop wondered how long he might have stood listening outside the door before knocking, and how much he had heard.

"Laborde sent me to ask if—" the barman began once more, and Bishop cut him off.

"Tell Laborde to keep his nose clean. This is none of his business."

"The hell I'll tell him that!" The doorknob rattled. "Why don't young Keller answer?"

"Because he's drunk," Bishop said.

"He didn't get nothing from my bar!"

"Would you expect him to drink your rotgut? Brought his own bottle with him. We'll sober him enough to send him home. Bonny, open that window and let's have some fresh air in here."

"You better bring him downstairs."

"Not till he's awake and can walk."

The barman retreated, making no attempt to muffle his footsteps, and clumped down the stairs. The barroom grew noisy with the entrance of several men, then Laborde snapped a word and the noise subsided. Outside in the yard, wood slammed heavily on wood. Bonny, at the opened window, winced.

"Sounds like they shut the gate! Shut us in!"

Red cocked an eyebrow at Bishop. "I much fear you've run the bluff as far as it'll go! Laborde won't wait long."

Bishop drew the door open and crept out along the passage, halting near the head of the stairs. He heard the barman saying below, "—groans stopped soon's I knocked. Damn queer, 'less Junior was sick."

"Or his bride," somebody suggested.

"Couldn't tell. They didn't let me in."

"What did Bishop say?"

"Said they'll bring Junior down when he can walk."

"Blow out the lamps," Laborde ordered. "We will be ready."

"If Bishop's troubleshooting for the Senior—"

"I don't believe it. Why the woman with him, and the redhead? I know that woman. I have a score to settle with her. We first make sure of Junior's safety. If any harm happens to him here the Senior will have me killed!"

"D'you reckon Bishop's trying to take him for ransom?"

"What else?"

Bishop returned to the room. Three pairs of eyes mutely questioned him. Shrugging, he let them know the worst

"Laborde's seen through the bluff. His first concern is to separate Junior from us, to save his own skin. His next concern, running a close second, is to get hold of Bonny. Alive, I take it."

"Could we blast out?" Red asked.

"The barroom's loaded with his crew. They've put the lights out. They could see us coming down those stairs, but we couldn't see much of them. You, me—maybe we'd make it. Just maybe. Or one of us. You're free to try."

"Leave Shamrock here? You're crazy! I'll never—"

Bishop cut Red short. "Forget it." Red's reaction was what he had thought it would be, yet its vehemence rubbed him the wrong way. It caused him to add in a roughened tone, "You've got no strings on Shamrock."

"Nor you!" Red flared. "Nothing gives you any right over her! It's your damned arrogance!"

His hard face darkening, Bishop stated, "I've been her guardian since the day she was orphaned. Not much of a real guardian, I admit. Bonny took that on. But still I'm responsible for her. And for Bonny."

"And I'm—"

"Forget it!" Bishop repeated. His anger drained as quickly as it had risen. He regretted having displayed it. Going to the window, he scowled at the barren skyline of Mexico across the river. Neither he nor Red owned any right over Shamrock. Damn it, the only man possessing that right was Junior, his malevolent enemy.

"His nerves are edgy," Bonny whispered. "He's worried. Not for himself."

Shamrock nodded. Red said, "Sorry I blew up." Then

to Bishop's back, formally, "I beg your pardon, Mr. Bishop."

The apology went wasted, Bishop asking abruptly, "Can you swim, Bonny?"

"Not a stroke. Never learned. Nearly drowned once when I was a kid, scared of water ever since."

From the overhanging window it was a straight-down drop to the river, slow-flowing, blackly sullen, its depth at this particular point unknown to Bishop. His swimming didn't amount to much, but he reckoned he might manage. Take a falling plunge and—barring he got stuck in the mud or broke his neck—struggle across somehow, possibly by holding his breath and walking on the bottom, weighted down by his clothes, boots, gunbelts and guns.

He had done the like before, as had many a hardpressed man of the dry country where swimming was a rare accomplishment, rarely needed. Load up for ballast and walk over. The rivers, such as they were, weren't wide. Red Mackenzie, being a wandering Scot, could no doubt dive in and swim this river. Shamrock could manage it.

But not Bonny. That was that.

Turning away from the window, Bishop raked his mind for a solution. He felt weary, dried out. His resourcefulness had reached exhaustion. His stomach growled. No food in—he couldn't remember how long. Nor rest, his sore muscles complained. He had skipped meals and sleep, hastening to be on time for Shamrock's wedding. Her wedding—God! How he had failed the kid.

He looked at Shamrock, at Bonny, and discovered that he was weakening in his strong instinct for self-preservation. The will to survive, that had carried him roughshod through countless scrapes, had dulled. It fell to second place. It was supplanted by the will to save those two, Shamrock and Bonny, at whatever cost. He judged himself responsible for them.

"Whoa, there!" Red pounced on Junior, who, recovering a tithe of consciousness, had begun crawling toward the door. "Stay put, you would-be lady-tamer!" Raising his face, Red looked at Shamrock. " 'Lady,' I said."

Shamrock's smile glowed, brilliant.

Junior flopped back onto the floor, clasping his head, mumbling threats. All parties concerned would die for this outrageous abuse upon his privileged person. All, he mumbled, viciousness vying with fear, unless they let him go. At once.

"My father is Mansell J. Keller! *The* Keller—the Senior! Goddam you, I'm his son! His son . . ."

Looking at him snivelling on the floor, babbling threats, Bishop felt a twinge of pity for him. Spoiled son of an ambitious and masterful father. The father had bred a weakling, a vicious young brute who strutted behind the power of the Keller name. The blame lay on the father for setting up tawdry standards of conduct, false values, evil examples. No ethical backbone. No rock-bottom code to sustain him in desperate straits. A pitiable young blackguard.

The shred of pity fled in the wake of a practical idea. "Bonny," Bishop said, "can you forget you're a lady? For just a few minutes?"

"Anything you say, Rogue."

"Can you act like a man?"

"Now wait a minute!"

"Do your best. You've seen men, plenty, sober and drunk and in-between." Bishop rolled the protesting Junior over facedown and began stripping him to his underwear. "Don't argue with me, Bonny! Take your clothes off and get into these!"

"But—"

"Do as I say, dammit!"

"Yes, sir!"

Bonny obeyed as if a trance, bewildered but taking

orders, for once cowed into docility—Bonny Belle Blue, one-time queen of the Blue Palace in Tombstone.

When she stood clad in Junior's wedding suit, Bishop surveyed her with serious misgivings. She was simply too much a woman to pass muster as a man. He stuffed her hair up into the beaver hat. Dissatisfied, he shook his head at her. The shape was wrong. She didn't in the least resemble a man. He had been a blind fool to imagine it.

"It won't do!"

"I tried to tell you," she said apologetically. "The clothes don't fit me. I'm no lady, but I can't help being a woman!" She hesitated. "It's a plain fact, Rogue. Plain as a fence."

"Plain as a sunrise, a rainbow, a rose," he countered, surprising himself. Colorful compliments did not come easily to his tongue.

He plucked the blanket from the strewn bedding on the floor. "Put this over you. Act shaky, like you've waked up with whiskey-chills and the flutters. Can't handle your liquor. But don't overplay it—you're not too sick to travel. Stumble a bit, so it looks right for you to lower your face and watch your feet, and hang onto Shamrock."

"It'll never work, Rogue! Not for you and Red, anyway."

"We'll give it a try. If we get split up, make for Naco."

"If? You know Laborde's not going to let us four—"

"Five," Red, said, hoisting Junior to his feet. "We don't leave this one here to bawl a warning!" From Bonny's discarded clothing he borrowed her voluminous cloak, draped it around Junior, and fastened its clasp under his chin. "Fair exchange is no robbery! Miss Bonny takes your place, and you take hers. Keep your mouth shut. Any guns that go off, mine"—he prodded the muzzle at Junior's ribs—"will be among the first!"

"All set?" Bishop asked.

They nodded. "See you in Naco," Bonny said, disbelief in her eyes.

Shamrock looked at Red and next at Bishop. "Be good, you two. Please don't get killed." She said it softly, and that was the woman in her. "Ornery big hounds," she added, and that was the O'Terran in her.

They left the room and paced the narrow passage in single file to the staircase. With all lamps dead, the barroom below appeared deserted. Not a sound came from it. The grime-filmed panes of narrow windows filtered gray light from the dawn-streaked sky, letting it fan in patches on the floor.

Gradually, men's standing shapes could be dimly made out, stationed motionless between windows. Backs to the wall, in deep shadow, commanding the staircase and the whole barroom, they waited. They had had time to accustom their eyes to the gloom, and the gray light seeped in from behind them, giving them all the advantage. A hoofstamp outside made itself heard distinctly in the silence. Bishop thought of his black horse and of Red's sorrel, tied up to the hitchrack out front.

"Laborde," he called, "I don't like your layout!"

"And I don't like your game," retorted Laborde. A single handclap sounded. The waiting men responded to the signal like a drilled platoon. Drawn gun-hammers clicked. "Come down, you and your partner and the woman. With your hands up! You're covered. My men are ready to shoot when I clap again!"

# XVII

The threat had to be discounted. It was Red who said, "You'll hit Junior! Can't you see he's in front of us, him and his bride?" Then answering his own question, "No, of course you can't. All cats look gray in the dark."

On the dark head of the staircase, above the reach of pale window-light, the five of them made a murkily seen group. The only distinguishable thing among them was the blue cloak. Unless he was insane, Laborde wouldn't give the second handclap, the signal for his men to fire up at the five, one of them the son of his master.

"Laborde—!" Junior began, and swallowed the rest, feeling the jab of Red's gun-muzzle.

"It's all right, Junior, don't worry," Red said soothingly, loudly, as if to a frightened drunk or a halfwit. "Laborde's made a mistake. Or else he's gone crazy—in which case we'll worry with you!"

"I know what I am doing," Laborde stated. But a trace of uncertainty crept into his tone. He dared not afford any mistake that endangered his credit with Keller. The mighty Hudson's Bay Company had long arms that relentlessly combed the world for anyone who absconded with Company cash. He had lost the cash. Keller was his protector, patron, master.

"As a sign of good faith, a proof you are not false," he hedged, "let them—Keller *fils* and his bride—come down!"

"That's what we're trying to do," Bishop said.

"Let them come down alone!"

"Oh . . . And we follow. No harm in that. Better not be! Junior don't feel well as it is. You'd have Keller

143

on your neck. By the way, you'll have to loan them horses. We've only got two, mine and Red's."

"Yes, I know."

Bishop touched Bonny and Shamrock lightly on their backs. "Hold onto your nerve," he whispered to them. "Laborde's got another trick. Play along with it and say nothing. Go on!"

He heard Bonny's sharp intake of breath, and shared her cruel tension. She was summoning her inner resources to combat her fear of Laborde, forcing herself to the frightful risk of detection. After that short hesitation she began the descent of the stairs, holding onto Shamrock and awkwardly bumping against her. She stumbled on an uneven step, looked down at it, and kept her face lowered as if the stumble made her more careful of her footing.

They proceeded on down to the floor. As they passed into the gray glimmer of window-light, Bonny shoved Shamrock forward and kicked her, causing Shamrock to trip onto one knee.

Bishop clenched his teeth. Was Bonny overplaying her part with that bogus act of ill-temper? He had drawn his guns when Bonny and Shamrock started down the stairs, in case of an upset. His eyes probed the gloom for a glimpse of Laborde.

Subdued half-laughter along the line of men applauded the act: Mean-drunk bridegroom asserting himself over his captive bride, whose bowed head tokened spirit-broken submission.

Bonny had played it right. She had succeeded in shifting attention off herself, in the gray light, and placing it on Shamrock. She had played convincingly the part of a brutal young blackguard, to an audience of blackguards. Playing it further, she caught Shamrock up by her disheveled hair and pushed her onward. The laughter mocked at pity.

At a word from Laborde, a man opened the front door for the pair and followed them on out. Bishop breathed a little easier. One crucial point was past, another coming up. Bonny must keep her face shielded from the man who went out behind her and Shamrock. It was lighter outdoors than in.

"How about those horses for the newlyweds, Laborde?" he queried. "Don't make them wait. Junior's in a hurry to get back home." He knew Laborde's answer in advance.

"No wait. They take the two at the hitchrack. The black and the sorrel."

"Those are ours!"

"Be glad," said Laborde. "Be glad to loan your horses to the son of Keller. You serve Keller, so you say." His tone dripped irony. "Your service to his son he will appreciate. I do you a favor, *non?*"

"Your favor sets us on foot," Bishop pointed out, equally ironic.

The workings of Laborde's mind could be traced. If Bishop and Red were false messengers, as Laborde suspected, then he had scored high credit by freeing Keller's son from them. If it should happen that they were genuine—well, Keller wouldn't bother himself about their personal troubles, as long as their troubles didn't inconvenience him or his son.

"This is a trading post," Laborde said. "We trade here for anything. We barter. We bargain fairly and keep true our word." Laughter rumbled again. He hissed it to silence. "I offer you a trade, Bishop."

"A fair bargain?"

"Most fair. Two good horses and liberty to ride out. For the woman—*M'selle* Blue of Tombstone!"

"Okay." Bishop had a ludicrous vision: Laborde finding that the blue-c'oaked person was Junior. "Clear the barroom. Call off your guns. Bring up the horses."

"You ask too much," Laborde reproved him. "First, send the woman down as proof of your good faith."

Outside, leather creaked and bridlebits jingled faintly. Hoofs struck the hard-packed earth. The man who had followed after Bonny and Shamrock came back in, reporting, "They're off. Funny thing, young Keller wouldn't let me—"

"No trade, Laborde—*you* ask too much!" Bishop rasped into the man's report, cutting it off. To Red, he whispered, "Back to the room! Take this fruitcake with you." Then the supreme insult, guaranteed to infuriate any French-Canadian and take his mind off other matters. "You're a cheap twister, Laborde, like all your goddam Canuck breed!"

A gun flamed. He expected it. You didn't smudge a man's racial pride, a pride as well-founded as anyone's, and not expect an instantly indignant repercussion. Laborde, thief and exile, his honor at zero, resented the sweeping slur on his blood lineage so much that it deprived him of cunning.

"Get them!" he rapped.

"Hold off a minute," demurred the man who had come back in. "I smell a trick! Something funny about how young Keller—"

Bishop fired off three shots and retreated along the passageway. If the man finished his sentence, it wasn't heard in the surge of commotion.

In the room, Bishop locked the door and wedged everything against it that was moveable. As a barricade, the pile couldn't block a determined assault on the door for long, but it would serve to stop bullets. The men were crowding up the staircase, cautiously slow by the sound of them.

Attempting a show of defiance, Junior sneered, "That won't keep them out! Laborde will skin you alive!"

Bishop sent him a baleful stare, and he cowered against the wall. "You're both crazy!"

"Quiet!" Red, listening at the window, pulled his head in. "The posse's coming," he told Bishop. "Can't tell how near. The river picks up the sound. The echo."

"Our friends on the stairs haven't heard it yet, then, in their own noise."

"The gate guards have, though. I haven't heard them open the gate yet to let Shamrock and Bonny out. Maybe I missed it. God, if we could only see the yard, see what's doing there!"

Bishop put his head out the window. As Red said, the river picked up the drumming of the oncoming posse, but the distance was hard to judge. "Are they holding them?" Red muttered, listening only for the sound of the big gate in the stockade fence. "It's taking too long to let them out!"

Time, Bishop reflected, had its measure in pain and joy. A minute of pain, of tearing anxiety, was an hour. An hour of snatched joy was a minute.

Wood banged on wood. The hoofbeats of two ridden horses started up and fell into rhythmic patter, the beat of loping, fading off in loose sand beyond the stockade fence. The gate had shut again.

"They got out! They're gone free, thank God!" Red's long minute of tearing anxiety was gone, too. He grinned at Bishop. "We put it over!"

His gladness wasn't wholly warranted, in Bishop's opinion, taking into account that their own lives lay precariously at stake. They turned from the window in time to catch Junior in the act of wrenching away the barricade, to get to the door. Red leaped and landed on him.

"No, you don't!"

The passageway resounded to the tramping of men who, finding it vacated, dropped their wary caution and advanced to the locked door. Junior began a yelp, which Red silenced promptly with a threateningly upraised gun barrel.

"What now, Mr. Bishop?" he inquired. "The river?"

"They'd break the door in before we got halfway across," Bishop said. "They'd pick us off, like shooting fish in a barrel." He meditated for a moment. "How good can you swim?"

"Pretty good."

"Then you go ahead. I'll wait till the posse shows up. It'll distract them. If Keller's with the posse, Laborde will be called on to explain things to him. That'll give me time to get out of here."

"It's a long chance!"

"Speaking for myself, so's the river."

Red shook his head. "Guess I'll wait with you."

"Suit yourself," said Bishop.

Somebody in the noisy passageway blasted the door lock, pointblank. The door gave way a few inches under pressure, then jammed against the barricade. With three shots in a close-space group, Bishop punctured a part of the door that was visible to him. The pressure ceased, and noise lessened, the men holding a muttering council before renewing the attack.

Outside in the yard, one of the men on gate guard raised a hail, calling to Laborde. Irritably, Laborde spat a command that hushed the muttering, and called back, "What is it?"

At the window, Red said, "I could tell him what it is! It's the posse."

The drumming of many horses swelled loud, then broke choppily, the Piety riders reining up to the stockade. Keller's voice rang out, brittle with impatience.

"Open up! I'm Mansell J. Keller!"

The massive gate crashed wide open for the riders to troop through into the yard.

In the crowded passageway the muttered discussion had ended. Laborde, downstairs and evidently hurrying out to meet Keller, threw back a word to his men, and they withdrew after him.

"Laborde! Ah, there you are. Where's my son?"

"He just left, Mr. Keller, with the young lady."

"Safe?"

"I made sure of that, sir." Laborde brought an obsequious civility to his tone, speaking to his master.

Contrarily, Keller's tone was arrogantly ungracious. "We thought we heard some shots. Why did you have all your men in the barroom? What's going on here?"

"A little trouble. Bishop—"

"Did he come here with a woman?"

"Yes, sir. And a red-haired man. I didn't trust them. They claimed to have a message for your son. True?"

"No! Are they still here?"

"I also made sure of that, Mr. Keller! They've barricaded themselves in an upstairs room, but we—"

"Have you got the river covered?"

"The river?" Laborde sounded surprised at the question. "And with the woman? They would be mad to try—"

"They'll try anything, you fool!" Keller blared. "Some of you men run round to the riverbank, fast! Shoot anything you see moving!"

Bishop didn't tarry to overhear any more. He regarded it as a finicky waste of time for Red to be tying his boots and gunbelt in a bundle with his bandana.

"Aren't you going to take your boots off?" Red asked him.

He shook his head. "Wouldn't help my kind of swimming." His only preparation was to stuff his hat under his coat, hoping to wear it again.

Feet hit the stairs, then the passageway. Red stuck a thumb at Junior. "What about him? He'll spill the trick. Shamrock and Bonny haven't had much of a start. Keller will track after them right away, won't he?"

"Bring him along. He'll do as a hostage, in a pinch."

"Okay. Lend me a hand."

Junior didn't appear to realize what he was in for, until they picked him up between them, bore him to the window, and unceremoniously tossed him out. He screamed, plummeting down headfirst. A splash, and he vanished, to reappear spitting and pawing, his head clay-plastered.

"He's lucky it's not a stony bottom! He doesn't know how to go into a dive." Red crawled out onto the window ledge. "Maybe he can't swim either."

He launched himself forward, arms straight and palms flat. He cut the water and rose farther on. Stroking back, he grabbed Junior and began towing him. Threshing in wild panic, Junior gurgled another scream.

Bishop pancaked, hitting the water a belly-buster that raised a mighty splash. As a dive it lacked style, but it met his purpose, which was to avoid repeating Junior's mishap. Air trapped in his clothes helped buoy him briefly while he swam half a dozen strokes before his boots and heavy gunbelts sank him.

He kicked bottom and rose to the surface. A gulp of air, a few strokes, and down he went. As a method of crossing rivers without a horse, it served in a rough fashion as long as the river wasn't too deep, the current too strong.

When he came up the third time, gunshots were exploding along the riverbank. Bullets lashed up little white fountains of water. Relinquishing the struggling Junior as a bad job, Red struck to deeper water and dived under. Bishop submerged.

# XVIII

Mansell J. Keller followed his men up the stairs, and in the passageway he rapped at them, "What's stalling you?"

"Something's jamming the door!"

"That you, Blount?" He had almost forgotten the sheriff, whose presence was contemptuously allowed only because it lent a stamp of authority to the gun posse.

"Get that door open!"

With help, Blount forced the door in. It was then that the firing broke out along the riverbank. Keller swore.

"They've gone!"

"Vamoosed," one of the men corroborated, looking through the doorway. "Took to the river. We'll get 'em, boss!"

"You better!" Keller stalked after Sheriff Blount into the room. He kicked at Bonny's discarded dress in the litter. "She stripped to swim, but where's her cloak?" A vague doubt, formless as yet, pricked his intelligence. "Her velvet cloak. She couldn't swim in that. She—"

"She's wearing it," said Blount, at the window. "No, she can't swim in it. She's wading back. Must be she can't get shed of it, or she's more modest than I thought. They've deserted her. There they go!" He whammed off two shots from his seven-load cylinder rifle, a .44 capable of tearing off a skull.

Keller looked over the sheriff's shoulder. "Missed! You don't shoot worth a damn, Blount."

"This rifle's for short range. In good light I can—"

"Let me have it!"

151

He snatched the rifle and pushed the sheriff away from the window. Carefully, he took aim at short range. The pupils of his eyes ballooned, then shrank to pinpoints. He thumbed back the knurled hammer to full cock, forefinger nursing the smooth trigger.

The bright blue cloak floated outspread like the giant blossom of a morning glory. The figure wearing it, head yellowed in clinging clay, face streaked, waded unsteadily toward shore.

Keller fired. He worked the hammer and trigger five times, emptying the rifle into the blue cloak. The wading figure sank without a cry.

"Good God!" exclaimed Sheriff Blount, horrified. "You killed her—murdered her!"

Keller turned on him savagely. "Shut your mouth! You ever let this out, you're dead! Understand? As dead as she is!" He gave Blount back his rifle. "She got caught in crossfire. Accidental death. You'll swear to it! Go tell Laborde to have his men pull her body out. She'll be buried in Piety."

Blount looked sickly at the rifle in his hands. The murder weapon represented his final degradation. Once an honest lawman, he had yielded to pressures, compromised with his conscience, gradually allowed himself to become so corrupted that Keller now expected him to sanction the coldblooded slaying of a woman. In an agony of revulsion he lifted the rifle to fling it away from him, to pitch it out the window.

Keller blocked him from doing it. "Pull yourself together! We're going after Bishop and Mackenzie!"

"I don't think they made it to the other side."

"Take some men and scout for signs of them. If you do find them, don't bring them back alive!"

Blount unpinned his badge. He looked at it, tipped his hand, let the worn old badge fall to the floor. "I'm finished taking your orders." His voice dragged tiredly. "Pick another sheriff."

"Do you know what you're doing?" Keller watched him move stoop-shouldered to the door. "Do you realize what it means?"

A heavy nod. "It means I'm finished. I should've ended it before this."

Red, getting across the river before Bishop, had won time in which to wring out his clothes and put his boots and gunbelt back on. "I took for granted you could swim," he mentioned, implying that he'd been mistaken.

Emptying his boots, Bishop growled, "How do you think I got over to this side?"

"It wasn't by what could rightly be called swimming," Red answered judiciously. "My conclusion is, you've got what's known in fancy language as a tremendous capacity for survival. Will power plays a part—or plain cussedness. Maybe that's it."

They had halted beyond the rise of the south riverbank, in brush too thin for cover, the rays of early morning penetrating it. Bishop stamped his feet into his boots. He sloshed his water-logged hat on. He was soaked, uncomfortable, and he clearly foresaw further discomfort, the discomfort of footsore tramping, hiding from pursuers, of thirst in the heat of the coming day.

One thing that helped mitigate his dour mood was the success of the trick, the substitution of Bonny for Junior. "Laborde doesn't know it," he said, "but he's due to catch hell from Keller." Then he thought of something else. "What did you do with Junior?"

"I had to turn him loose."

"Then Keller knows by now."

An animal-cry rose from the river behind them, a cry of wrenching, horror-stricken despair. Red nodded somberly. "He knows! I wouldn't wish that on any man, not even Keller. You didn't see what I saw."

"Speak plain! We don't have much time."

"We'll have time, Mr. Bishop. I started back for Junior. Thought he was drowning."

"More fool you! So?"

"Keller came to the window. The room window. He fired a rifle down at—at Bonny's blue cloak. Murdered his son, thinking it was Bonny. He'll live in a worse hell than he can deal to Laborde! A lot worse. If he lives with it. If he doesn't go mad some night and kill himself."

Bishop shook his shoulders. Future hardship shrank to a minor matter. "Well . . ." A tremendous capacity for survival. Will power. Or plain cussedness. Whatever it was, it worked, it bore him through. "Let's mosey while we can."

"Where?" Red asked.

That was better. It set the mind to work. "South, there's thick brush, then badlands. Barrancas. West of the barrancas it's high range. I know a *ranchero*. Name's Alarid."

"The bandit?"

"*Ranchero*, I said. You say the same. He'll give us horses."

"How far to his hideout? Pardon, his *rancho*, I mean."

"About eighteen miles, more or less, depending on what route we have to take. And rough going most of the way. Especially the barrancas."

Red examined his boots. "It's a helluva roundabout way of getting to Naco. Not much choice, though."

"We'll get there," Bishop said, "sooner or later. Once we're in the high brush we can throw off any trackers."

"I hope those two wait for us in Naco."

"They'll wait."

They were waiting. They both came dashing from the Naco Hotel & Saloon as Bishop and Red clopped up the main street. Bonny, still wearing Junior's clothes, raised a greeting arm. Shamrock uttered a glad squall that brought townspeople out to stare at the girl in her old canvas pants and flannel shirt; at the woman in male attire; at the two hardworn and unkempt riders. A scandalous foursome. Birds of a feather . . .

Red swung down off his horse. Without a word, he grabbed Shamrock to him.

Bishop touched the brim of his hat drawling, "Good afternoon, ladies! Are you particular about the kind of company you keep, or would we do?"

"I guess you'll do," said Shamrock, her eyes saying much more.

"They look mighty rough to me," Bonny demurred. "Downright disreputable. Wonder where they stole their horses? Mexican saddles, I notice. Oh, well—we might do worse. Do you gentlemen have any money?"

Bishop nodded. "Some."

"We'll let you pay our bills, kind sir. Hotel, restaurant, livery. They're getting pushy. Began hinting we'd have to work ourselves out of hock. Your saddle's up in our room."

"I'll get it."

The bar served as the hotel desk. "The ladies are checking out," Bishop said. "Give me their bill."

"Ladies?"

His stare froze the sneering bartender. "D'you want the rent, or a bust in the jaw?"

"Sorry, mister! The rent."

He paid the bills at the restaurant and the livery stable. "Them gals—" began the liveryman.

"The ladies are leaving. Bring out the black and the sorrel. Now! And they better be in top shape."

Naco watched the disreputable four depart. "Tombstone," Bonny sighed. "I should've stayed there. The gamblers and hotshots, I always got on fine with them. They even respected me. But these upright citizens! Upper crust! Piety. They sharked me, smiling to my face."

"Let it be a lesson," Bishop responded. "Our kind cheat on the level."

"That sounds funny, but it's a fact."

Red said to Shamrock, "I'm heading out for California. Would you—?"

"Try and stop me!"

"The trail forks off about a mile from here."

"We'll take it!"

"Shamrock!" put in Bonny. "It's disgraceful! Remember, after all, you're a married lady!"

"She's neither married, nor, strictly between us, a lady," Bishop contradicted. "Her husband met with an accident. A fatal accident. No," he said, "it wasn't my doing, Bonny. Nor Red's. It was somebody else. Made a mistake—fired at your blue cloak. Junior was wearing it. Killed him."

"God!" Bonny breathed. "Keller?"

"Accept my condolences, Shamrock. You're a widow."

Shamrock thanked Bishop absently, her mind on higher things. Red was telling her frankly that he was flat broke and on the run. Laying it straight on the line, he was no bargain. Trouble dogged his heels. He often went hungry.

"Get to the point, Red," she interrupted his confession of his shortcomings. Her eyes sparkled. "We'll have a glorious time together, broke or in the chips!"

Unbuckling the straps of his capacious and bulging saddle pockets, Bishop remarked to Bonny, "If you'd looked into these you could have paid your bills."

"I don't search men's pockets. Did you rob a bank?"

"Depends on how you look at it. After I throttled

Keller senseless at his office window . . ." He paused. "Didn't I tell you? Well, then I took his keys. Went into the bank, unlocked the vault, collected your money and jewelry."

They gaped speechlessly while he pulled wads of banknotes from the saddle pockets.

"There might be enough here to cover the cost of your house, too. I didn't have time to count it. By now, Keller knows his vault's empty. Empty as his life," he ended, and felt a twinge of pity for Keller. That black-hearted man, broken and ruined, would creep out of Piety some dark night, abandoning the wreck of his would-be empire. If, as Red had said, he didn't kill himself.

Bonny recovered her voice. "Rogue, you devil—give Shamrock and Red some of that money, will you?"

"A pleasure."

Red shook his head. "None of it's mine, Miss Bonny. It's yours."

Shamrock nodded agreement. "You've done too much for me, Bonny, you and Rogue." She played her eyes over Bishop's face. "I still love you, Rogue. I always will. But not in—in that silly way I used to—"

"I know," he said, giving her a rare smile. "You've got Red. He'll do." Youth to youth. He crushed a sense of loss. She would trek with Red to California, forever out of his life.

"A wedding present," Bonny insisted firmly. "Rogue, peel off a thousand and make them take it. Make them!"

"That reminds me—" Bishop dug into a saddlepocket. "I brought you a wedding present, Shamrock. For your Piety wedding. It'll do for the one that's coming."

Gravely, he gave it to her. It was a silver box, daintily engraved, set with turquoise stones. An elegant trinket, fit to grace a lady's boudoir. A jewel case.

"I put some knickknacks in it for you. Lost the key, though. You can open it later with a hairpin."

Shamrock, eyes misty, stroked the silver box. "Thanks. I'll take good care of it all my life, amigo."

Amigo. Friend. Nothing more of young, hot affection, infatuation. Endless absence would dim the memory. "Maybe Red can use it to keep his tobacco in," Bishop said.

In a short while he said, "There's the fork. Don't give us any goodbyes. Don't look back. Red, get rid of that sorrel and buy another horse. With a bill of sale. Don't forget to marry your girl somewhere along the route to California."

He and Bonny watched the pair take the northwest fork, riding closely side by side. Bonny shook her head mournfully.

"They're so wild! What will become of them?"

"Don't you worry about them," Bishop cheered her. "What I put into that silver box was a wad of these greenbacks. Stuffed it full. Didn't figure you'd mind."

"Of course not."

"That pair of madcaps are made for each other. They'll kick up their heels, high, wide and handsome. For a while. Until the babies start coming. They they'll settle down somewhere and raise a family. Red's a Scot, the kind that respects responsibility, once he takes it on. And Shamrock's no featherhead. In a few short years we wouldn't know them. Solid citizens."

"There's a lot to be said for family life," Bonny observed presently, in pensive mood. "I never had it." Her gaze traced lingeringly Bishop's strong profile. "Might be tempted to try it, if—"

He promptly changed the subject, asking her, "How're you feeling? I mean your health."

"Pretty good. It's a wonder, after what the old doc said about my heart. He must've been wrong."

"It was probably indigestion. Moping in that damned town, you sank into low spirits and nervous flutters. You're not cut out to be a lady of leisure, any more than Shamrock. It wasn't your kind of life."

"You're dead right, Rogue. The devil with it!" She began to sparkle. "Tombstone, here I come!" She kissed her hand at the wide sky. "I'll open up a bigger and grander Blue Palace, by golly, and I'll live again!"

Bishop nodded. "Okay. But it's two days' ride. This is rough country for you to ride alone, carrying a fortune in cash and jewels."

"I was thinking the same thing!"

"So I'll travel with you—"

"Fine!" She flushed with pleasure.

"—as far," he said, "as the outskirts of Tombstone."

**L(eonard) L(ondon) Foreman** was born in London, England in 1901. He served in the British army during the Great War, prior to his emigration to the United States. He became an itinerant, holding a series of odd jobs in the western States as he traveled. He began his writing career by introducing his most widely known and best-loved character, Preacher Devlin, in "Noose Fodder" in *Western Aces* (12/34), a pulp magazine. Throughout the mid thirties, this character, a combination gunfighter, gambler, and philosopher, appeared regularly in *Western Aces*. Near the end of the decade, Foreman's Western stories began appearing in Street & Smith's *Western Story Magazine*, where the pay was better. Foreman's first Western novels began appearing in the 1940s, largely historical Westerns such as *Don Desperado* (1941) and *The Renegade* (1942). The *New York Herald Tribune* reviewer commented on *Don Desperado* that "admirers of the late beloved Dane Coolidge better take a look at this. It has that same all-wool-and-a-yard-wide quality." Foreman continued to write prolifically for the magazine market as long as it lasted, before specializing exclusively for the book trade with one of his finest novels, *Arrow in the Dust* (1954) which was filmed under this title the same year. Two years earlier *The Renegade* was filmed as *The Savage* (Paramount, 1952), the two are among several films based on his work. Foreman's last years were spent living in the state of Oregon. Perhaps his most popular character after Preacher Devlin was Rogue Bishop, appearing in a series of novels published by Doubleday in the 1960s. George Walsh, writing in *Twentieth Century Western Writers*, said of Foreman: "His novels have a sense of authority because he does not deal in simple characters or simple answers." In fact, most of his fiction is not centered on a confrontation between good and evil, but rather on his characters and the changes they undergo. His female characters, above all, are memorably drawn and central to his stories.